# LIKE A BOSS

## DOUBLE TROUBLE DUET - BOOK 1

LIZ MATIS

Little Hondo Press

Contact: littlehondopress@yahoo.com

Like a Boss – Double Trouble Duet – Book 1

Copyright 2017 Elizabeth Matis

Digital ISBN: 978-0-9908848-6-6

Print ISBN: 978-1974552535

Photo and Cover Design by: Sara Eirew Photographer

Editor: Finish the Story

www.lizmatis.com

elizabethmatis@gmail.com

Sign up for my newsletter www.lizmatis.com

# CHAPTER 1

*D*awson shoved the last customer out the door and into the waiting cab. He slipped the driver a twenty and headed back to the bar.

He'd named the dilapidated building the Last Chance Saloon because it was his last chance at having a place in this world. Most would call the bar on the outskirts of the Alaskan town a hole-in-the-wall, but it was his hole-in-the-wall. So what if it wasn't a place 'where everybody knew your name'? That was the way his patrons wanted it, anyway. Along with its owner, the shabby interior mirrored the souls he served.

Rather than let the bar ripen, he grabbed a mop and set to cleaning the floor. The military had quickly cured him of his slovenly teenage ways. He didn't mind the manual labor. In the predawn hours while the world slept, he was at peace.

Finished, he counted the cash and smiled at the uptick in sales.

The door opened with a bang. The cold, summer, morning air blew in, setting off the heater. He cursed himself for not locking up.

"Sorry, bro, we're closed," he said, not giving away how his hand gripped the gun he kept by the register.

"How did you know it was me?"

Dawson looked up. Even though he hadn't seen his brother since they were twelve, there was no mistaking his twin. Born physically identical in every way, but raised by separate parents, they were as different as night and day. Abel and Cain.

They were a classic study of nature versus nurture with nurture winning by a landslide. Aaron, who'd been raised with wealth, was clean-shaven even at five in the morning, had a neat haircut, and was impeccably dressed. Dawson, raised by a heroin addict, sported a shoulder-length mess, a beard that any biker would be proud of, and wore jeans and a T-shirt that read, *DOGS – Because People Suck.*

But no matter how much he tried to disguise himself, there was no hiding from the gaze that greeted him in the mirror every morning. The same eyes stared back at him now.

And for that, he hated the man who, despite a slight limp, walked toward him with confidence only money could buy. The suit probably cost more than the night's receipts. No, Aaron wasn't there to rob Dawson, not of the cash anyway. He'd already taken their father, and along with him, Dawson's pride. What was there left to take?

He itched to draw the pistol on the pompous prick

as he bellied up to the bar like he owned it. Instead, Dawson slipped his hand from the gun to a glass, and then poured Aaron a shot of his cheapest scotch. "I hope you don't need one of my kidneys, because you're shit out of luck if you do."

"No, but I do need your help."

"The billionaire needs my help? Oh, the fucking irony."

"Look, I was boy then. How was I supposed to react?"

The day his mother had dragged him across the Canadian border to meet the father he'd never known and a brother who looked exactly like him should have been the greatest day of his life. "You were an asshole."

"If I could take back that 1 day, I would."

Dawson studied his twin, but he couldn't get a read on him. Was the billionaire using his negotiating skills to get what he wanted, or did his brother really regret his actions? Either way he was curious, not that he planned to help him. "I'm listening."

"I need you to be me for thirty days."

*Thirty days?* Dawson noted the bloodshot eyes, drawn and shallow skin. Realization dawned. "Rehab?" He eyed the drink he'd just poured.

Aaron's grip tightened around the glass. "Not what you think. The alcohol was liquid courage to face you," he admitted. He looked away, then back. "Pain pills."

Most couldn't afford their addiction or get a doctor to write a script and turned to cheaper alternatives like heroin for relief. With his billions, his brother could get anything he wanted. Hell, he probably had a doctor on his payroll.

"What happened? Get a paper cut?"

"Rock climbing accident. Shattered my leg."

"And I'm supposed to give a fuck?" Trouble was, he did. A little. Dawson cursed his younger self for wanting a relationship with his twin.

They should have been switching identities as kids. Playing pranks in grade school and sharing girlfriends as teens. And now his estranged brother wanted Dawson to pretend to be the CEO of King Enterprises. "No way."

"If the shareholders find out I'm in rehab, stock prices will freefall. I'll be ruined."

"Poor little rich boy."

"Dawson, don't make me beg."

But that was exactly what he was going to do. Make him beg like his mother had begged their father for drug money. Except her poison had been straight-up heroin.

His father had offered his mom a payout, and in return, they'd crawled back across the border. Within two years, she was dead of an overdose. After that, Dawson bounced from foster home to foster home until he turned eighteen and joined the Army.

Yep, no fucking *Parent Trap* happy ending for him.

"What do I get out of it? I have a business to run."

"You call this shit hole a business?"

And this piss ant wanted his help? Dawson stretched his arms out, placing his hands on the bar, and leaned in. "At least I worked for what I have."

Aaron stood, then mirrored the pose, their foreheads almost touching. "You don't think I work hard?"

Dawson nodded to the manicured nails across from him. "No. I don't."

Aaron sat back on the barstool and smiled. "If that's what you think, then taking my place should be a cake walk." With a smug look, he added. "And at the end, you'll have a million dollar paycheck."

"Fucking cheapskate. You're a billionaire."

"Ten million."

"No."

"Twenty million." Aaron downed the scotch and winced. "Fuck, that is godawful."

"Some people can't be bought."

Aaron nodded for another pour. "Then donate it to some charity."

Fuck. He had him there. Dawson could do a lot of good with that kind of money. Maybe even start a program to help out the homeless veterans living in the alleyways of downtown. He helped when and where he could, allowing the men to wash up in the bathroom and doling out peanut butter and jelly sandwiches before opening to the public in the afternoons. And if he could locate his former military service dog, he'd have the funds to fly Boots home now that he was retired. "How do I know you'll uphold your end of the bargain?"

Aaron reached into his suit jacket pocket. "Contract," he said, tossing it on the bar along with a pen. "I already signed it."

Dawson flipped to the last page. Aaron King. Seeing

the last name that should've been his, too, twisted his gut. *For fuck's sake, get over it!*

"I'll have my lawyer look at it." Not that he had one.

Aaron shook his head. "No one can know about this. Don't worry. My company is too important to me to risk screwing you."

Like father like son. Dawson gave the contract a cursory read to make sure he wasn't signing away his rights to some sort of inheritance. Not that he'd accept it, but he wouldn't let his brother swindle it out from underneath him, either. The old man was still alive anyway. Not that he kept tabs. Much.

He noted an advanced of a million dollars and the remaining nineteen payable in thirty-one days.

"How did you know I'd accept the twenty?"

"Bro, you're my twin."

Dawson wanted to punch the shit-eating grin off of Aaron's face. Reaching the end of the document, he deemed everything on the up and up. His brother was risking his business while, with an upside-down mortgage on the bar, Dawson didn't have a pot to take a crap in and had truly nothing to lose and everything to gain.

He scrawled his name at the bottom. Dawson Trudeau.

Aaron frowned. "You'll have to practice my signature, among other things." Pulling out his phone, he continued as he scrolled. "My assistant, Lacey, will instruct you in all you need to know."

"Your assistant? Is she part of my fringe benefits package?"

"Hands off. She's worth more to my company than any quick fuck."

"You mean our company."

A look of concern flitted across Aaron's face. "For thirty days."

Dawson enjoyed baiting his twin with a not-so-reassuring grin. "Of course."

Aaron froze, no doubt having second thoughts, but then a feminine voice answered.

"Please tell me he said no."

"I won the bet, Lacey. Come meet your new boss."

Dawson heard a string of expletives emitting from the phone. It didn't sound like she was on board with the switch-a-roo. He wondered what she'd lost on the bet. Despite her sexy first name she was probably a frumpy assistant doing his brother's dirty work. *And I just agreed to do the same. Fuck.* Now Dawson was the one having second thoughts.

How the hell had his twin tracked him down, anyway? How much did he know? "In case you're wondering, Mom's dead."

Aaron belted back the liquid and dropped the glass to the countertop so hard that it should have shattered. "As far as I'm concerned she always was."

Dawson's hand fisted, but he couldn't say he blamed Aaron. Dawson felt the same way about the sperm donor.

The door flew open, and a gorgeous redhead walked in, instantly brightening up the dingy bar and the dark places in his heart. Wearing a lavender pencil skirt and matching blazer, she wasn't dressed for the chilly summer Alaskan morning. With sky-high heels, she belonged in L.A. with his brother. Yet, Dawson couldn't squash a feeling that she belonged with him instead.

Her eyes, green as absinthe, had the same effect as downing a shot of the powerful brew, which was why it was a moment before he realized they were looking at him with disgust. So what if she preferred men like his metro-sexual brother? It would be his pleasure to change her mind. Aaron had warned 'hands off', but he should have added an addendum to the contract. Because there was no way Dawson wasn't going to fuck her. And it wouldn't be a quick one.

At least his rough appearance didn't seem to scare her.

It should. They say never judge a book by its cover, but in his case Dawson came as advertised. Hard. Every inch of him.

# CHAPTER 2

*L*acey Brooks schooled her features to hide her shock. The beast behind the bar couldn't be Aaron's twin brother.

Shaggy. Unkempt. Rough.

She'd been expecting her boss' mirror image, not someone who'd crawled out of the Alaskan bush. But as she drew closer, she could see there was more than a resemblance underneath the beard and past-the-shoulder length mane.

*Never trust a man with longer hair than you.*

*Never trust a man period.*

Keeping his brother a secret from the world was one thing, but how had Aaron managed to keep it from her?

She knew everything about the CEO of King Enterprises. *Everything.*

Lacey wasn't just his assistant, she was his confidant, his therapist, his sometime tennis partner, and his friend. But if he'd kept this secret, what else was he hiding? Like the reason for the cloak and dagger maneuvers, which he'd dismissed as unimportant.

Was it a family feud? A scandal?

Or was Dawson dangerous? A criminal? He certainly looked like it. His icy blue gaze roamed her body as if he owned it, reminding her of Aaron right before he was about to close a deal—a predator. Not like a shark, for they attack on instinct. This was more like a wolf toying with its prey before sinking its teeth into the neck of its dinner.

"Lacey, I'd like you to meet my long lost brother, Dawson."

"I look forward to working with you, darling."

*Darling? Ugh.*

*That twangy accent? Double ugh.*

The physical makeover would be the easy part. Taming the he-man into a sophisticated owner of a billion dollar corporation in a day would be impossible.

She wasn't a miracle worker even if Aaron called her Saint Lacey on a daily basis. And it was a miracle she'd gotten Aaron to agree to rehab. Only the threat of her going public with his addiction spurred him into getting help.

"My name is Miss Brooks. Not darling, not babe, not sweetheart, or any other sexist name."

"Oh, you are a redhead through and through."

Trouble was, he was right. Lacey had a temper and a smart mouth to go along with her red locks. Perhaps if she went blond her temperament would sweeten? It wasn't a problem around Aaron, who had a calm business demeanor and treated her with respect.

"Cool it, bro," said her boss. "King Enterprises doesn't need a sexual harassment lawsuit marring its reputation as an equal opportunity employer."

Lacey considered herself fortunate to work for the company *Forbes* had named one of the top ten places for women to work. Equal pay and stellar childcare, not that Lacey had need of the latter, but maybe one day.

Dawson held up his hands in mock surrender. "Ok. I'll behave."

Lacey doubted that. She would have her hands full babysitting Dawson while running King Enterprises.

"How soon can you be ready? We're taking the jet to the headquarters in L.A., then Mr. King will be leaving for Costa Rica as soon as the jet is refueled."

Dawson folded his arms. "Doesn't sound like rehab to me. More like a vacation."

She tore her gaze away from the raw power of his inked biceps. Bad boys were her weakness. She was just like her mother, only Lacey would never abandon her career to follow her loser second husband and let him gamble away her daughter's college fund on a 'sure thing'. No way.

Hopefully, once Dawson was shaven and shorn and clothed in one of Aaron's suits, her libido would take a nosedive. Damn, would the CEO's clothes even fit?

*Great, another thing I have to stress about.*

She winced as Aaron picked up the glass. Going

into rehab hungover wouldn't be an auspicious beginning.

"It's some kind of holistic, new age bullshit." He knocked back the contents.

"It's not bullshit. And it's far removed from the prying eyes of the press." Lacey defended the facility she'd chosen. More importantly, it was far removed from her boss' supply line and enablers.

"Give me fifteen minutes," said Dawson.

Once the door closed to the backroom, Aaron swiveled the bar stool to face her. "Do you think he can fool everyone?"

Lacey couldn't tell Aaron the truth. Couldn't tell him that his brother wouldn't get through the first day on the job, never mind thirty days. If she did, then he wouldn't go to Costa Rica to get clean. The employees of King Enterprises depended on him. She depended on him.

He could be a ruthless businessman. Sometimes, a little too ruthless. A little too greedy. But to his employees, he was generous. All he expected in return was hard work and loyalty. She would pull this off, even if she had to drag Dawson out of the dark ages.

He walked out of the backroom. His hair combed back into a bun. Lacey despised the hipster look, but he rocked the man bun like a warrior on the *Game of Thrones*. She battled between the urge to cut it off and to let it loose so she could run her fingers through it.

"All set."

As Lacey turned, and her heel caught a rut in the wood planking of the floor. One brother caught the left arm, and the other caught the right. Only one touch burned through the sleeve of her blouse. Thankfully, the cool Alaskan air doused the spark.

Before leaving, Dawson slapped a makeshift sign on the front door.

*Closed for renovations*

Before Lacey could stop the insult, it flew out of her mouth. "You might be better off razing it to the ground and starting over."

His eyes narrowed. "Maybe you should go lighter on the perfume."

Her mouth dropped open, and she turned to Aaron for backup.

Her boss shrugged. "Too bad it's not masking the godawful smell out here."

Lacey wrinkled her nose. "Yeah, what is that?"

"The real world."

Apparently, the real world smelled like piss and vomit.

They rode to the airport in uncomfortable silence. You'd think the two brothers would have something to talk about. Even a, 'What's up?' would be welcomed at this point. Lacey was glad she was driving, even if Dawson had taken the seat next to her, his clean citrus scent not offensive in the least.

Once aboard the jet, the stalemate continued.

The silence stretched, and valuable time ticked away.

She negotiated multi-million dollar deals on Aaron's behalf, but navigating this sibling rivalry looked like it would take a whole different skill set.

"Mr. King and Mr. Trudeau." With both of their gazes now trained on her, her mouth went dry. "Um, you might want to use this time to prepare for the switch." She grabbed a pad and pen from her purse and thrust them into Aaron's hands. "Why don't you start with the signature while you talk, so your brother can pick up your speech patterns. Hopefully."

"Your faith in my abilities overwhelms me," said Dawson, with his drawl kicked up a notch—probably just to aggravate her.

For the next hour, the two brothers worked together. Though no deep down feelings were exposed, no fists were thrown either. She considered it a win.

"Miss Brooks, do you think I sound like Aaron?" asked Dawson.

Lacey looked up from the latest financial report. "Passable." Actually, it was fairly good, but she wasn't about to tell him that. "Just keep your mouth shut as much as possible."

"Jesus, Lacey, I've never seen this side of you," said her boss, his gaze curious and assessing at the same time.

"Jet lag." She didn't add that *she* was the one who was supposed to be jetting off to a tropical island on vacation. She hadn't taken a day off in two years. "Dawson doesn't know the company. The less he says, the better."

"What about dear old dad? Surely, he'll suspect," said Dawson.

*Oh boy, here we go.* At least both brothers had the

same lockjaw like tic. It was rather fascinating that they'd both developed it.

"Father is semi-retired and currently with his twenty-year-old whore in Monaco," Aaron answered.

The silence, and the tension, returned.

Lacey sprung up. "Perhaps you should try on one of Aaron's suits to make sure they fit?" She escaped to the back of the plane that held a bed and a closet. She returned with a classic, navy pinstriped suit that her boss kept onboard.

"Trying to get me out of my clothes, Miss Brooks?"

Lacey wouldn't doubt if her cheeks were as red as her hair. "There is a bathroom."

"No need. I'm not shy."

*Well, neither am I.* She didn't look away from the strip tease. Okay, so inside her head it was a strip tease, complete with music and smoky lights.

"Sorry," said Aaron. "I'll give you combat pay for putting up with him."

She put her hand on her hips. "Twenty million?"

Between Dawson's throaty chuckle and imagining what he packed underneath those black, Calvin Klein boxer briefs, her own panties dampened with slick heat.

Ever the negotiator, Aaron offered, "50k and a promotion. How does Vice President sound?"

It sounded amazing. Still, it wasn't twenty million. "V.P. of what?"

"Of the world, obviously," butted in Dawson as he struggled into the suit jacket.

Lacey bit back a smile. Then bit on her lip as she

realized the jacket would have to be let out. She made a mental note to call the tailor. Aaron kept in shape with a personal trainer and a nutritionist, so his muscle tone was more sinewy than Dawson's brawny frame. Hopefully, no one would notice the difference. But she certainly did.

Worse, Dawson noticed her noticing him as he shed out of the button-down shirt, nearly tearing it at the seams. She knew she should look away but couldn't. She added a pack of new dress shirts to her growing to-do list.

"I think I'm going to like being the boss of you, Miss Lacey."

*Miss Lacey?* Dawson was baiting her on purpose, but she wouldn't give him the satisfaction of biting. She had to let him know who was boss. In a calm and even tone, she said, "You've got it wrong, Mr. Trudeau. For the next thirty days, I'll be telling you what to do and how to do it."

$\mathcal{T}$he thought of Miss Strawberry Shortcake bossing him around in the bedroom made him go rock hard. *What the fuck?*

He called the shots in and out of the bedroom, steering clear of domineering women. Especially redheaded vixens. Gingers were trouble. Evil.

Trouble was, his cock didn't care. Dawson turned away before Lacey dropped her gaze and got an eyeful.

"Jesus, bro," said Aaron, then busted out in laughter.

Dawson slipped back into his jeans and tried to tuck and stuff his cock into a comfortable position, making his brother lose it even more.

"What's so funny?" asked Lacey, her hands fisted on her hips.

Aaron faked a cough, using his fist to cover his mouth. "You don't want to know."

Lacey tapped her foot. "I think I do."

Zipped up, Dawson turned to face her. The outline

of his erection pressed against his jeans. "What he's trying to say is that we're identical in every way."

Lacey looked confused.

"Size wise," Aaron added.

She looked down at the bulge in Dawson's pants, causing his cock to painfully twitch a 'hello there.'

Her brow rose. "You're right. I didn't want to know."

But judging by the way she swept her tongue along her bottom lip Dawson thought that was a lie.

"I'm going to catch a couple of hours of sleep before you two whip them out and compare them like three-year olds."

"Sweet dreams, shortcake." He'd certainly given her something to dream about.

Once the door closed, Aaron grew serious. "She'll get you through this if you let her."

The respect in his brother's eyes for his assistant was admirable, but how did his twin keep his hands off that body of hers? Dawson guessed money was more important to Aaron than scoring with his assistant— yet another way in which they were polar opposites.

If Dawson wanted his twenty-million-dollar payday then he better stop lusting like a brute and start learning how to be a cold-hearted businessman like his brother. "What's next?"

"How about a long, boring history and run down of the company?"

Dawson knew some of the information from the Internet, not that he kept tabs. Much. Aaron wasn't kidding that it was boring as shit, so he pretended to be in a war room briefing, listening intently like his life depended on it.

Only it was hard to concentrate knowing Lacey was horizontal on a bed just a few feet away with only a flimsy door between them. He fantasized about waking her when it was time to land and itched with jealousy when Aaron did the honors.

Only Aaron gave a polite rap on the door, opening it, but not stepping in. "We're landing," he said, and then returned to his seat.

A moment later, Lacey emerged with her clothes rumpled and her eyes glazed with sleep

After the click of the seatbelt, she smoothed back her hair. She glanced at Dawson, and a blush bloomed on her face before averting her gaze. Had she dreamed of him? Of Aaron? Both? *Gross.*

He'd never thought about it from a woman's perspective. A fantasy of sexpot DD sisters doing him was ruined forever.

The plane touched down, and Dawson grabbed his backpack. Before he could take Lacey's overnight bag, Aaron swooped in.

"I'll walk down with you. I need some fresh air while they refuel."

Stepping onto the tarmac of the private airstrip, Dawson wouldn't exactly call the L.A. air fresh. The blast of heat caused the familiar rising of his blood. His hackles rose, ready for a fight. Claws scratched at the walls of his throat as he tried to drag in a breath.

He spun his head around to take in the scenery, grounding himself in the here and now. He wasn't in

Afghanistan, but squinting against the bright sun only made it worse.

"I'll just wait in the car."

The female voice behind him jolted him from the terror before it's tendrils could snake it's way around his heart. He turned around to see Lacey take her bag from Aaron and walk away.

Damn, her ass had a hypnotizing sexy sway. And he was back. Now that was a cure he could get behind. Literally. And the only side effect was a hard-on. Dawson laughed.

She turned around, and his gaze snapped up, but she wasn't looking at him.

"Aaron, don't worry. I'll take care of everything."

"I know you will."

Lacey glanced Dawson's way then headed for the Lincoln Town Car outside the small hangar.

His brother put out his hand.

Dawson eyed the gesture with skepticism, but he relented. They were physically identical except for their fingerprints, yet this formal, business handshake summed up their relationship: two people at opposite ends of the deepest chasm of the Grand Canyon. Brothers should hug it out. High five. Fist bump.

"Don't screw this up," said Aaron, tightening his grip.

"Me? I'm not the one going into rehab."

A flicker of hurt flashed in his brother's eyes. Dawson didn't regret his words. He wasn't going to let his twin treat him like shit—not even for twenty million dollars. Being rich didn't make him better than anyone, it only let him rehab in Costa Rica instead of a jail cell.

The silent power struggle continued, each vying to make the other flinch first.

"I meant what I said about Lacey."

"Are you in love with her?" He needed clarity on this before he pursued her. Dawson had never actually agreed to the stipulation to keep his hands to himself.

"She's my best friend." Aaron let go of his hand. "Truth, she's my only real friend."

Yeah, well Dawson didn't have any friends. Except for his customers, no one would notice he'd left town. And that was just fine with him. Friends disappointed you. Died on you.

Yet, as his brother hit the top of the stairs, Dawson offered an olive branch. "Hey, Aaron."

His twin turned around. "Yeah, bro?"

"Get well."

"Just don't get too comfortable in my chair."

*Prick.*

By the time he walked to the car, he'd shrugged off the sting of Aaron's dig. That's what he got for hoping for reconciliation. For a family. *Idiot.*

Dawson slid into the passenger seat, ready to lighten his somber mood. "Guess it's just you and me, shortcake."

By the way her hands tightened around the steering wheel, Dawson knew she was pissed. Good. He'd keep her that way—mad like a good little redhead. He'd rather see anger in her eyes than a lust he couldn't resist stoking.

Though if he truly desired revenge against Aaron, he'd go out of his way to charm Lacey into his bed. But Dawson didn't play games. He wasn't his father's son or his brother's brother.

If he went after her, it would be because he couldn't stay away.

"My name is Lacey. In the boardroom, I'm Miss Brooks. Can you remember that?

"So, Miss, huh? Not married, good to know."

"I have a boyfriend."

"No you don't. You're married to the job. Perhaps have a thing for my brother?"

"I do not! We have a strictly professional relationship. And so will we." She nodded her head as if she was trying to convince herself.

"Then he's an idiot. Or gay. And I'm neither."

"Doesn't matter which he is, or which you are. I'm not interested. In either."

"He inherited the billions, but I got the looks."

The lilting sound of her laugh hit him in the gut.

"You're identical twins."

"Yeah, I got screwed." As much as he loved to make her mad, he loved her smile, her laugh, even more.

"Once this is over, you'll be a millionaire. Have you thought about what you're going to do with the money?"

He shrugged, not willing to admit that after paying off the bar, all of the money was going to build a veteran's homeless shelter in his adopted hometown. "Not really."

On the drive, she talked non-stop, filling his head

with more information about King Enterprises than he needed to know and then ran through Aaron's routine. Which seemed to be work from dawn to dusk, and Dawson was more of dusk to dawn creature.

"Any questions?"

"Any girlfriends I should know about?"

"No one serious."

Maybe he'd finally live his teenage fantasy of sharing girlfriends with his brother. And having a woman to entertain would keep him distracted from Lacey's strawberry lips. So damn kissable, when she wasn't talking.

"Which brings to me to…well…you must be celibate for the next thirty days."

Where did she come up with that? Aaron only said to keep away from her. "Want me all to yourself, do you?"

"Hardly. Your tattoos will give you away as Aaron doesn't sport any. Besides, it would get complicated."

"No sex? I think I deserve a bonus." In truth, it had already been more than thirty days since his last time.

"Sorry, it's already part of the contract."

"Well, hell. Damn that fine print," he said.

Her laughter was like a pop song, making him feel light and at ease.

They arrived at an estate situated on the hillside. The post-modern style of stone, metal, and glass was unlike the brick mansion he'd visited as a child. He whistled upon entering through the huge copper doors.

"I'll show you to Aaron's bedroom." Lacey walked up a few stairs off to the right.

Dawson stood rooted to his spot in the large foyer, and not because of the view of the city that lay beyond the infinity pool.

"Bedroom? That's not a good idea." Despite his teasing, he'd try his best to honor his brother's wishes.

When she whirled around on the step, he caught her gaze and lost his breath, knowing his best wouldn't be good enough.

"Why is that not a good idea?"

Lacey was either naïve or dense.

"Because I'm not a saint like my brother."

"Believe me, your brother is no saint." She trailed her delicate fingers along the curved teak banister, and he imagined what it would be like for her to touch him in the same way.

Before he could ask her to elaborate, he heard a discreet cough.

Dawson turned toward the sound.

"Egads, how dreadful." A distinguish older gentlemen had popped out of nowhere. "Are you sure you're the same boy who darkened the halls of King's Manor?"

"I remember you," said Dawson. "Edward, right?" The King's butler looked the same—very old. Dressed like he stepped out of the 18th century, he was out of place in the postmodern space. Dawson remembered him ruffling his hair and calling him, 'my dear, boy' and the kindness he'd shown. Another person ripped away from him.

Bitterness he'd thought he conquered spilled out of his mouth. "Did Aaron inherit you, too?"

"Dawson, that was uncalled for!" Lacey breezed by him to give the butler a kiss. "I was just about to show him Aaron's bedroom."

"Dear, I can see you've had your hands full. I'll take it from here."

"Thanks, Edward." Lacey spun on her heel. "I'll be here in the morning at six. Be ready," she ordered.

"Have the coffee ready. Industrial strength." Dawn to dusk—Dawson would be living on coffee and energy drinks for the next thirty days.

"Let's get something straight. I'm not your secretary, not your maid, not your cook, and not your sex slave."

"Sex slave? Now why did you have to go and put that delicious thought in my head?"

Her smile could only be described as triumphant. "Sweet dreams, Dawson." With a flip of her hair, she left like she knew his dreams would be anything but sweet.

Edward clapped his hands together. "Let's get you shaven and shorn."

Dawson might look like an animal, but damn if he'd be treated like one. Ready to tell the butler off, he turned, but he stopped when he noticed Edward smiling.

"Still the angry boy, I see. You and Aaron have more in common than looks."

What the hell did his brother have to be angry about? Not getting a pony for Christmas?

Dawson followed him up the stairs, down the hall, and into Aaron's bedroom. He had one nice thing to say for his brother: he had impeccable taste. The hardwood floors gleamed in the sunshine flooding through the walls of glass. He'd give anything to crash on the platform king-sized bed.

"Through here."

Dawson was led to a masculine, wood-paneled bathroom with all the amenities you might expect a billionaire to possess. The barber chair was a surprise.

The butler snapped a black cape and looked at Dawson expectantly. Despite having second and third thoughts about changing his appearance, he plopped onto the chair.

Without a moment's notice, Edward unceremoniously snipped off the man bun.

*Fuck. No going back now.*

After five more minutes of using a clipper to finish up the cut, Edward tugged at Dawson's beard. "I need a machete to hack my way through this. There's nothing nesting in there, is there?"

So what if his face hadn't seen a razor in five years? Dawson wore his beard with pride. "I can do it myself."

Edward rolled his eyes. "No sense of humor, just like your brother."

Being compared to his twin, especially in a negative way, soured his stomach. Questions burned on his tongue, but they went unasked as Edward went to town on his beard like Edward Scissorhands. A hot towel to soften what was left followed, then the scent of lemon filled the air from the balm applied to his whiskers.

"How bad is Aaron's addiction?" When the butler hesitated, Dawson added, "He's my brother."

Edward nodded. "I suppose if he trusts you to run his company then…well…he collapsed but still refused to get help. Miss Lacey threatened to go public. I don't think that scared him as much as your father finding out."

That was telling.

"And he trusts you to not say anything to your employer?"

"Your father fired me even though I served this family for forty years. I won't go into the details. Aaron hired me back with health benefits. And for that, I will forever be in his debt."

Dawson eyed the wicked-looking razor in Edward's grasp, but his wizened hand was steady. Still. Perhaps being in Aaron's debt included offing the spare heir. He went to object, but the butler spoke first.

"Now, this works much better if you're not talking." After a few minutes of scraping and a stinging smack of aftershave, the butler unsnapped the cape. "The tailor will be up shortly."

"Thank you, Edward."

"Your welcome, Mr. King," he said with a curt nod, then left him alone.

*Mr. King.* Once upon a time, he'd have given anything for that last name. Now he was being paid twenty million to pose as Aaron, the boy he grew up hating. Had he made a bargain with the devil? Or did he and Aaron have a common enemy?

He slid off the chair and walked to the vanity. Dawson peered into the mirror, hating the reflection. Without his armor of hair, more than his face was stripped bare.

Every sin of his past was etched across his face like a road map to hell.

# CHAPTER 4

$\mathcal{T}$he next morning, Lacey sat in Aaron's chef's kitchen, pounding out a memo on her iPad, stabbing at the keys, pretending it was Dawson's head. She'd specifically told him to be ready at six. She hoped this wasn't a sign of the way the next thirty days would unfold. Unsettled from a restless night of dreams filled with her fingers exploring the labyrinth of Dawson's abs, she was the one who needed the extra fifteen minutes of sleep, not him.

Though she'd rather have coffee, she took a sip of tea in an attempt to calm her growing agitation over being kept waiting. Besides, if she made coffee, it only would've added fuel to Dawson's notion that she was just a secretary.

"Miss Brooks, I need you to take a letter," said a clipped, authoritative voice.

Lacey looked up and down, did a double take, and nearly spilled her tea. Wearing a classic, navy blue,

Armani business suit, he looked exactly like Aaron. *Idiot, what did you expect? They don't call them identical twins for nothing.*

Hope welled inside her. Perhaps they could pull this off.

Yet, there *was* something different. It was in the eyes. They were the same shape and the same sapphire blue, but Aaron never looked at her with lust the way Dawson did. She wore a to-the-top-of-the-collar, buttoned-up blouse, yet he saw right through her shield of clothing.

If only she wasn't attracted to him, then she could block anything Dawson threw at her. Trouble was, she wanted to answer the 'call of the wild' look in his eyes. Hoping a bitchy attitude would put him off, she let annoyance taint her next words. "I thought we covered this. I'm not your secretary."

"Assistant, secretary...same thing."

"It is not. I'm Aaron's right-hand man."

He leaned across the counter. The scent of citrus and leather aftershave infiltrated her senses and defenses. What would it feel like to trace her fingers where his beard had been?

"But you're a woman," he whispered, his minty breath a cool breeze caressing her heated cheek as he pulled away.

At the moment, she was well aware she was a woman. Her naughty parts thrummed with anticipation as if her seat vibrated like a missile at Defcon One.

"Yes, well." She stumbled over her words, then

30

straightened in her seat and added with a burst of confidence, "That's why shit gets done."

His smile was different, too. Unlike Aaron's tight-lipped grins, Dawson's mouth curved into a sexy, slightly crooked, half-smile.

"I see. I am woman, hear me roar," he said.

Oh, she wanted to roar all right. Dawson's fiery gaze promised that and more. She'd thought once the beard was gone and his tats were covered, he'd essentially be Aaron and she'd be immune. After all, when they'd met at Harvard, she couldn't stand him. While her student loans ticked up like the National Debt Clock, Aaron reeked of white-boy privilege. As she got to know him, however, she admired his intelligence and work ethic. At his company, Aaron was all business, all the time. And yes, he still reeked of money, greed, and entitlement. Perhaps all good attributes for a billionaire, but not for a husband.

On the opposite side, there was Dawson, uncivilized and untamed. He invaded her personal space. Acted like she existed merely to please him and for him to please her back.

"And you're a male sexist throwback to the Sixties."

"You're wrong about that. I've served with too many kick-ass female soldiers to ever be that."

In an instant, her theory was blown. "You were in the Army?"

The smile left his face, replaced by a mask of stone. "Shouldn't we be going?"

Had he'd been dishonorably discharged? Suffer from PTSD? Instead of answers, she had more questions. The way he'd shut down she knew better than to ask. Damn Aaron for not trusting her with the whole story. How was she supposed to operate without all the information?

She took her frustration out on Dawson. "Like twenty minutes ago."

Lacey slid out of the seat and led him to his brother's seven-car garage. "Can you drive a stick? Aaron takes the Lamborghini out on Mondays."

Dawson whistled like he'd seen a bombshell blonde instead of a garage full of hot rods.

"One...two...he has a car for every day of the week?"

"Yes," she said evenly, hiding the resentment she felt over Aaron's extravagances. She knew the value of a dollar. Even though he paid her extremely well, she had a modest home and a six-year old sedan. Lacey didn't just save for a rainy day; she squirreled away money like a category five hurricane was bearing down on her life.

She held on as Dawson sped out of the driveway. Hopefully, at this speed at least, they'd miss the L.A. traffic. Otherwise, they'd go from being early to being late.

While he drove to the office per the GPS directions she'd set, she concentrated on answering emails—hers and Aaron's. She had double the work when she should be on vacation, sleeping off a hangover from one too many colorful umbrella drinks. Between the extra hours and keeping Dawson in line, she'd earn every penny of the promotion her boss promised.

"Did you hear from Aaron?"

"Oh." From the way they'd treated each other, she was surprised Dawson cared enough to ask. "Yes. Just to say that he arrived. They'll be taking all his electronics—which for him will also be a sort of rehab." She smiled to lighten the mood.

"What's your vice?"

*Wine, chocolate, bearded men with tattoos.* "I don't have one."

"Everybody has at least one. Let me guess. Shoes?"

"Now that's sexist."

"Not if it's the truth, it's not."

"Well, it's not." Rather than admitting to her vices, including her collection of Beanie Babies, she bounced the ball back into his court. "What's your?"

"Redheads." He rubbed his chin.

Was he missing the beard, or did his skin itch from shaving it off?

"That's not a vice, per se."

"It is when you can't help but count the ways you could please a certain redhead."

Now that had delicious possibilities. Unfortunately, she was on a starvation diet until this was over. She'd be too busy to even think about sex, never mind have the energy to find out how high he could count.

She directed him to the underground parking garage of one of the tallest buildings in L.A., and then to the spot reserved for the CEO. She dug through her purse for the credentials he'd need as he pulled in and turned off the ignition.

"This is Aaron's backup phone. It has all his

contacts, but please let all incoming calls go to voice mail. I'll review them every few hours and give you a script to read if you have to call back."

He nodded, turning it on. "What's the code?"

"1225." Lacey slid out of the car, juggling her purse, tablet, and tea mug.

"Our birthday? He might as well not have a code."

"Don't blame me. I've tried to get him to change it." She slammed the door with her foot.

At the entrance to the private elevator that shot up to the headquarters of King Enterprises, Lacey handed Dawson his entry passkey. He swiped it.

Before she'd been nervous that he wouldn't pass for Aaron. Now, she worried that he would, and with the keys to the kingdom, Dawson had the power to rule. Had her boss made a wise decision by entrusting his estranged brother? Perhaps the painkillers had dulled the part of Aaron's brain that processed information. Could Dawson be trusted with a billion dollar company?

Her Google searches on Dawson Trudeau had turned up nothing, nor was he on any of the dating or social media sites. Seriously, did you exist if you didn't have at least one social media account? I Facebook, therefore I am?

Except for the standard Yellow Pages listing, not even his bar, with the highly original name of Last Chance Saloon, had any hits. The man was a ghost.

And it wasn't like she could ask Human Resources to do a background check. If they ran across his photo, the family's thirty-two year old secret would become public information.

So how the hell had Aaron found him?

Dawson wasn't the talkative type—at least when it came to himself. When it came to having an opinion on something, it seemed like she couldn't shut him up. And that could lead to trouble.

He held the door open for her. "Um, coming?"

"Remember what I said on the plane?"

"That you're not shy?" He raised a questioning brow.

Of course, he'd remember something like that. "No, the less you say, the better."

"Yes, boss lady. I do remember," he said with a hint of a smile.

That hint made her yearn to discover his secrets even more. And not because she was worried about King Enterprises.

CHAPTER 5

*A*s he walked the halls of King Enterprises with Lacey in the lead, Dawson dwelled on what his life could have been. Instead of benefiting from the privilege and security his brother enjoyed as a boy, Dawson had known the burn of hunger and the helplessness of watching his mother shoot up. As soon as he'd turned eighteen, he'd joined the Army. Facing gunfire, sweating through grueling days of heat, and spitting sand was easy compared to that. But watching good men die took its toll on the hard shell he'd honed during his childhood years, chipping away at it until he knew he had to get out. To save his sanity. To save his soul.

What kind of man would he have been if the tables had been turned? What if he had been the firstborn? Would he be like Aaron in other ways besides looks? Edward pointed out how similar they were, but

Dawson wasn't a spoiled, metro sexual, greedy, moth-erfucker like Aaron.

Would the twenty-million-dollar payday change Dawson? Not likely. He was giving most of it away. The devil on his shoulder nudged him, *"You should keep it all. You deserve it."*

*"Fuck off,"* he told off the devil with language he could understand.

The sooner the thirty days were over, the sooner he could put this behind him. Dodging bullets was more luck than skill, but faking his way through the next month would take everything in his arsenal. He'd talked his way out of tougher situations than posing as a billionaire. It was all in the attitude. The tailored business suit he itched to shed was his uniform for the mission. The haircut, shave, and the last minute mani-cure were all part of the role he had to play.

Lured again by the hypnotizing swing of Lacey's hips, he followed obediently through the mazes of offices and cubicles. Accounting, Marketing, Research and Development, Human Resources. *Ha!* If they could read his mind at this moment he'd be sent to HR like a naughty boy sent to the principal's office.

*Lacey's naked hips rocking back and forth on top of me, instead of the side-to-side sway she'd mastered like a forties movie star.*

The employee handbook probably had a policy against sexual harassment. But it wouldn't be harass-ment if she approached *him*. Now that would be a turn-on. He had to figure out a way to make it happen. As a last resort, he could shred the employee handbook and throw the resulting confetti over Lacey's naked body.

"And this is where Dottie sits. She comes in at eight."

She turned, breaking the spell her ass had cast. Or perhaps it was a hex.

"Up here, Mr. King."

He met her gaze, and instead of apologizing, he smiled.

"This isn't going to work if you keep leering at me."

*Leering?* He didn't want to be *that* guy. Dawson decided to be on his best behavior, though he did his best work when he was bad.

"And this is Aaro...I mean your office." Lacey threw open the mahogany double doors engraved with an emblem of a crown. The billion-dollar view from the top floor probably made Aaron feel like a god, never mind a mere king. Two seats in front of an ornate desk made of the same wood as the doors, a computer, and an executive chair, along with a credenza, filled up the right side of the room. A conference table with six chairs and a burgundy leather couch made for an afternoon nap—or something even more pleasant—took up the left side.

The idea that Aaron and Lacey might have used the couch for that something more pleasant turned Dawson's stomach. Aaron had said they were just friends, but maybe they were friends with benefits.

On further inspection, he noticed that no file folders were strewn about. No paperwork to be pushed. What exactly did his brother do all day? "It doesn't look like much work gets done in here," he commented.

"As a military man, I'm sure you appreciate neat and orderly."

All these comparisons to Aaron grated on his last nerve. He was nothing like his brother. And Dawson's tidiness wasn't so much a result of the being in the Army, it was from not having much as a kid.

Drawn to the freedom of the outdoors, he walked over to the bank of windows to gaze out at the L.A. skyline. The morning sun mixed with smog created a yellowish hue that hung over the city. He already missed Alaska, his home since leaving the Army two years ago.

"Look around and familiarize yourself. Your private bathroom is through that door. I'll be right back."

A moment of panic hit his gut. What if someone came in while she was gone? He walked over to the desk and spun the chair. His gaze fell on the credenza. Funny how Aaron's house had no photos, but here, where he worked, he kept a timeline of his life almost as if it were just for show.

Dawson gritted his teeth as he witnessed the life that should have been his, too, played out before him.

A photo of ten-year-old Aaron and their father fishing off a yacht.

At the beach.

At DisneyWorld.

High school graduation. College graduation—Harvard. Of course it was Harvard.

What was Dawson doing here with his pitiful high

school education?

He could speak five languages, diffuse a bomb, knew land navigation and terrain association like his life depended on it—because it had.

But none of that mattered in his brother's world.

He snickered at the photo of Aaron jumping out of a plane. *Pussy.* Try a HALO jump with fifty plus pounds of gear. Another photo of his brother heli-skiing. So his brother liked to live dangerously. A tour of Afghanistan would've cured him of that. He heard the door open.

"Good morning, Mr. King, I'm sorry I'm a little late. Here's your tea," said a woman. *Dottie?*

*Fuck, where is Lacey?* He didn't know if he could do this alone. But hell, he'd walked his whole life alone, what difference should this day make? Behind him, he heard the clink of the cup on his desk. Here was the big moment.

He desperately needed a fortifying breath but turned without taking one. "Good morning, Dottie. Thank you."

Even with an old-fashioned name, he expected Aaron's secretary to be a hot number, like Lacey. Instead, a woman who had to be in her sixties, stared back at him as if he had two heads—or as if he wasn't Aaron. *Fuck. She knows.*

"Is there anything wrong, Dottie?"

She smiled as if surprised. "No, no, nothing is wrong. You're welcome, Mr. King."

If he'd taken that deep breath, he would've expelled it in a whoosh of relief. He'd passed the first test.

# CHAPTER 6

*I*n the office she rarely used, Lacey took deep cleansing breaths. The exercise usually calmed her. Centered her. Not today. Instead, she thought she'd pass out from sucking all the air out of the room.

She'd tried numerous times to teach Aaron the breathing technique to reduce his stress and help with the pain in his leg. He'd rolled his eyes and wondered out loud how such a sensible woman could believe in such crap.

So she knew he wasn't going to be happy with the facility she'd enrolled him in, which focused on a holistic approach to rehab. Forget a vice president position—she might be out of a job, period.

Deep breath. *Whoosh.*

And thirty days of working with Dawson? She felt like she was the one who'd done something wrong. *Or something right.*

But the question remained. Could King Enterprises trust him? Could she?

She picked up the phone, thinking Edward might be privy to the family secrets. He'd been the butler for the King's since before Aaron—before the twins —were born.

"Good morning, Miss Lacey. How's our boy holding up?"

*Boy? Our?* Which one? "Hi, Edward. So far so good. What's the deal between our boys? Why were they raised separately?"

"Mr. King didn't tell you?"

This time she knew exactly which one he was talking about. "No." She paused. "There wasn't enough time before he left," she lied. That Aaron hadn't confided in her didn't hurt, it angered her.

"I'm afraid I can't disclose family business."

"Please, Edward. I need to understand what's going on. Can Dawson be trusted?"

Edward sighed. Lacey pictured him shaking his head.

"You've been put in an impossible situation, but like you, I signed a confidentiality agreement. Besides, I only know a small part of the story. There are always two sides and then the truth."

Lacey tried a different approach. "Did you know Dawson was in the Army?"

"No, but it doesn't surprise me."

"Why?"

"The way he carries himself. The beard. The tattoo. Has Special Forces written all over it."

*Special Forces?* Perhaps Dawson deserved the benefit of the doubt. "Sorry to bother you, Edward." She hung up no wiser than a minute ago, but at least the butler seemed to trust Aaron's decision. Grabbing some files she'd need for later and her Wonder Woman mug, she left the office in search of caffeine.

As she rounded the corner to the employee break-room, she heard Dottie's voice.

"I think he's drunk."

*Oh no.* Had the secretary delivered the boss' morning tea?

"Who's drunk?" Lacey asked brightly, as if nothing was amiss.

"Mr. King. He said good morning and thank you. And didn't say a word about me being late."

The three other women with Dottie stayed on as Lacey poured a cup of coffee. "That doesn't mean he's drunk." Aaron rarely touched alcohol. One of those exceptions had been in Dawson's bar, which told Lacey just how far Aaron had fallen. "There could be a million reasons why he's acting human."

"He's been replaced like one of those pod people," said a nerdy girl from Accounting.

That was too close to the truth. Thank God, she wasn't in the process of taking a sip, otherwise, she'd be wearing coffee on her blouse for the rest of the day.

"Stroke?" suggested Amy from Human Resources.

A new hire, not knowing their boss at all, said, "In love?"

But Dottie nodded in agreement. "That must be it.

Lacey, you know him best. Is there someone?" Her tone hinted that Lacey was that someone.

She knew about the constant speculation about her and the CEO. With spending so much time together, how could there not be? But hers and Aaron's relationship was a purely professional one.

Like her, he had no social life. Everything revolved around his company. From dinners to tennis matches, he was always working some business angle.

Clearly, though, she didn't know Aaron at all. Certainly not about his addiction—until she'd found him unconscious in his office—or about his secret brother. Geez, for all she knew, her boss had a hidden sex playroom in his house.

"His business is his mistress," she said, adding a splash of whole milk to her mug, wishing for something stronger. "Speaking of which. Mr. King doesn't pay us to gossip."

By the time she added a packet of sweetener, she was alone in the breakroom. Sometimes she hated being management. It would be nice to be one of the girls for once, instead of the office killjoy. She downed half the liquid black gold like a shot of tequila. Fortified, she was ready for the day. And for Dawson.

Passing by the secretary on the way to the CEO's office, she smiled as a peace offering. "Sorry, Dottie."

"Don't be sorry. I shouldn't have spoken out of turn. Especially in front of the others."

"Thanks. We're working on an important project and can't be disturbed for any reason." The less interaction between Dawson and the staff, the better. She swung open the office door and shut it behind her.

"About time. I thought I'd blown it with Dottie." From behind the desk, Dawson skimmed a hand across the top of his head. Lacey was sure he was looking to tug on the missing length.

"I heard. She thought you were drunk." She crossed the room to the conference room table. Before placing her mug down, she took another long hit.

"What the hell did I do to make her think that?"

"Mr. King is a generous employer, but, well, your brother can be curt at times. Please and thank you isn't part of his vocabulary."

"That doesn't surprise me."

"And then you didn't say anything about her being late. Aaron abhors tardiness."

"Is that why you were in a snit this morning?"

She dropped the files on the table with a thud. "A snit?" Her voice rose, and she strode back to the desk where Dawson sat, looking like he belonged there, wearing an amused look that she wanted to wipe off his face. Or kiss off.

"Whoa, I take that back." He held up his hands in surrender. "Lacey, I promise I won't tease you about being my secretary but you're going to have to sneak coffee in here for me. Tea is for pussies."

She gritted her teeth. "How do you like it?"

"Diesel."

Her gaze landed on his powerful chest. No amount of tailoring could hide the strength beneath the suit or erase the image of his tattooed biceps in her mind. Heat bloomed in her blood. "No cream or sugar?"

"Are we still talking about coffee, Lacey?"

*No.* "Yes."

"Too bad." There was no mistaking the disappointment in his voice.

Thankfully, he changed the fiery vibe in the room by clapping his hands and rubbing them together like a villain out of a silent film. "What's first? Takeovers? Extortion? Bribery? Evicting little old ladies?"

"That's not what King Enterprises is about," she defended. Upon reflection, remembering some of the shady deals that Aaron had agreed to against her advice, she mumbled, "Much." She walked back to the table, took a seat, and opened her laptop, ready to dive into the pile of work. "I was able to cancel your meetings, so there's nothing you have to do."

"I can't do nothing."

"Your job today is to look pretty." She smiled sweetly, taking such gratification in the statement.

"Too easy, babe. I can do that standing still."

She'd let that one slide but only because she knew he was trying to get a rise out of her and not because the endearment created a hum of excitement that a modern woman shouldn't feel. "Then do it taking a nap." She drained what remained in her mug.

"Great idea." With a sarcastic, side-eyed glance, he added, "Especially since I still don't have coffee."

Lacey glared at him as he walked by. Stretching out on the couch, he reminded her of a lion readying himself for a nap.

His brow shot up. "Care to join me?"

She snapped her gaze back to the screen. Though sleep sounded like heaven, she knew Dawson had a different version of heaven on his mind. "I'll pass."

With his eyes closed and his mouth shut, she was able to concentrate on work. But once his breath deepened and evened, her gaze lifted to study his features.

The lines on his face had smoothed, and the chiseled cheekbones softened. His lips—so kissable when he wasn't speaking—called to hers. In the past twenty-four hours, she'd restrained herself from strangling his corded neck, but now she imagined nuzzling her nose there to breathe in the scent of his skin.

His expression darkened as if he were fighting something. Instead of using her fingers to type on the keyboard, she wanted to use them to caress his brow and ease whatever he was dreaming about. Or reliving.

She craved to snuggle up against his hard body. Have his arms snake around her, holding on tight as he fought whatever demons haunted him.

Then he started to snore, waking her from the daydream she wove with such clarity she almost thought it was real.

Coffee. She needed more coffee. And since she'd rather have him awake and annoying than sounding an alarm throughout the building with his snoring, she'd get Dawson a cup, too.

*Black. No cream. No sugar. No me.*

# CHAPTER 7

*D*awson woke with a start, his gaze darting around the room for Lacey. He hadn't planned to nap, but the tapping of her fingers on the keyboard and the whiff of her intoxicating perfume had lulled him to sleep.

Sitting up, he checked the time on the Rolex Daytona Platinum watch on his wrist, admiring its ice blue dial. It was a thing of beauty. A small greedy part of him echoed a desire to buy one for himself. But since it cost more than the average American worker's salary, the larger part of him could never justify the extravagance, especially when a ten-dollar watch could tell him that forty-five minutes had gone by. The grogginess from the lack of sleep haunted him. *That's a lie.* It was the memories that dogged him.

If God existed, then the least he could do was answer one simple prayer and have Lacey bring back the nectar that was coffee.

He stood, stretching out his tight muscles before pacing the floor. Being lazy wasn't in his creed. Relaxation? What was that?

Doing nothing would drive him crazy. He eyed Aaron's computer and figured what the hell. He switched it on and sat on the throne of the family dynasty. The screen for the user's password popped up. If the code for his brother's phone was anything to go by, then hacking his computer would be child's play.

*A password usually requires at least eight characters. At least one capital letter, one number, and a special character.*

The number part had to be the same as the phone. And most people began with a word. He tried King@1225. *Incorrect password.* After two more failures, he looked around the office. Settling on the Harvard Diploma, he typed in Harvard@1225.

*Bingo.*

He pulled up the Internet and signed into his personal email to see if he'd received any messages from the guys about the hunt for the team's retired service dog. With no new messages, he brought up the website that helped veterans adopt the dogs they served with.

The door flew open, and Dawson's stomach dropped. Had he triggered a security breach by incorrectly logging in too many times?

A tall, beautiful brunette barged into his office with a world of confidence. He recognized her from somewhere.

He stood. "Can I help you?"

Dottie was hot on the woman's heels, which was saying something for the older woman.

"I'm sorry, Mr. King. I told the reporter you were indisposed." Dottie came to stand between them, as determined as a mama bear protecting her cub from a wolf.

"Samantha Jameson, Mr. King. We were scheduled for today, but I didn't get the email that you had canceled."

Now he knew why she looked familiar. From reading her heartbreaking book, *Broken Arrow*, Dawson doubted her claim. She'd gotten the notice and ignored it.

Her story had transported him back to the battle-grounds of Afghanistan and Iraq, and by the end of her story, he'd respected the hell out of her. Soldiers weren't the only ones who suffered from PTSD. That explained why she was now a sports reporter. That didn't explain why she was here.

"It's okay, Dottie. I'll squeeze her in."

Perhaps he should wait for Lacey to return, but she'd blow the reporter off. Dawson could take care of this himself. Besides, he was bored.

"Sorry, Dottie," said Samantha as the secretary left.

"Hmph."

Dawson had a feeling he was going to catch hell from his employee for not supporting her. He didn't blame his secretary.

"Take a seat, Ms. Jameson." Even though she was married to the former pro football player, Ryan Terell, she'd kept her byline.

"Mr. King, thank you for seeing me. Finally."

Dawson hid a smile. "I loved your book."

She arched an eyebrow as if she didn't believe him. "You read my book?"

He nodded. "I'd love to talk more about it, but I'm on a tight schedule. How can I help you?"

"Rumors are flying that King Enterprises is vying for the New York Kings."

*The football team?* "I can't confirm or deny that. We do have very diverse holdings." There, he sounded like an executive.

She sighed like she knew what his answer would be all along. "Theoretically, would you be interested?"

"Theoretically, it would be a great branding opportunity. King Enterprises—the King's football team—I can see how people would think I'd be interested."

"Would you move the team to L.A.?" The reporter was trying to trip him.

"And share the same name as the hockey team?"

"Vegas?" she suggested.

Lacey walked in, holding two mugs. "Ms. Jameson, Mr. King has an appointment."

"Yes, well, so did I," Jameson said over her shoulder before returning her gaze back to him. "One more thing. If you read my book, then you know about my husband's charity, Jenny's Cure?"

Dawson did remember. "Say no more. Leave the details with Dottie, and I'll get a check out within the week." The company had to have a charitable donation line in its budget. If not, he'd tell Lacey to take it out of his twenty million. Or pawn his brother's fifty thousand dollar watch.

Jameson stood, and so did he.

"Thank you, Mr. King."

As the two women crossed paths, he half-expected, half-wished for a catfight to start. Instead, a look of respect passed between them.

"Well played, Jameson," said Lacey.

"A girl's gotta do what a girl's gotta do."

The door closed.

"What were you thinking?" Lacey hissed.

"Giving away money or talking to a reporter?"

"Both! You could have blown it."

"I think it went rather well." Dawson repeated the conversation. "Now, please tell me that one of those is mine."

She nodded but said, "I can't leave you alone for a moment." Instead, of placing the coffee down, she rounded the desk.

Their fingers brushed. If he hadn't been prepared for the zing of awareness, he would have bumbled the handoff, as she clearly wasn't ready for whatever her body was feeling. Their gazes locked.

Oh ho-lee hell, it was like a hit of morphine.

Lacey looked away first, doing a double take when she did. "How did you get into Aaron's computer?"

He eased into the chair and took sip of the coffee. "Too easily. You'd think a Harvard graduate would be smarter."

She leaned across him to hit a key to wake the screen. In doing so, she woke up something else as well. The curve of her hip to her ass begged for a man's firm grip. He shifted in the chair.

"Did you do anything?

The rising panic in her voice insulted him. "What? Like wire money to my off-shore account in the Grand Caymans?"

The screen came to life. A moment passed before she looked back over her shoulder. "You're going to use the money to find your service dog?"

"Well, not the whole twenty million." He smiled.

"I'm…I'm sorry for thinking the worst."

An apology? He didn't even know what that sounded like.

Lacey drew herself upright and turned to lean against the desk. She folded her arms and looked down. "What's your dog's name?"

"Boots."

"Boots?" Lacey laughed. "That's adorable."

The sound lifted his heart.

So he wasn't about to chance ruining her mood by revealing that the dog's full name was Puss 'n Boots and it had nothing to do with his white paws and everything thing to do with 'boots on the ground' and the pup's tendency to sniff women's crotches.

"Yeah, well, ISIS didn't think so. He was so good at sniffing out bombs they had a bounty out on him. Once his current handler was killed, he refused to work. Dogs get PTSD, too."

"I'm so sorry. I hope you find him," she said gently.

Too gently. Like apologies and how his heart beat faster when she drew close, he didn't know how to handle it. He needed the other Lacey back. "Enough small talk. Back to work, slacker," he said.

She glared at him. Now that he could handle.

The rest of the day dragged on until finally Lacey shut her laptop and said, "Let's call it a day."

"Good." Despite doing almost nothing and taking a nap, he was exhausted. "Let's get some dinner."

"We are, Mr. King, at a charity dinner. Tux required."

He hated hearing his brother's name spoken from her lips. When he and Lacey had sex, and they would have sex—it was inevitable as the oncoming sunset—she'd say, "Pretty please, Mr. Trudeau." By the end of the night, she'd be shouting *Dawson* at the top of her lungs.

Though attending a charity function was the last thing he wanted to do, at least he'd be able to spend time with Lacey instead of rambling through Aaron's home, feeling like an intruder. "What time should I pick you up?"

"I'll come get you at eight."

"A gentleman doesn't let a lady 'come get him.'"

"We are equals."

"By that logic, since you picked me up this morning, I'll pick up you tonight." He had no problem being equal with a woman in the workplace—or in the bedroom. If she wanted him to be the one screaming her name, then so be it. And with that delectable mouth, Lacey would be the woman to do it, of that he had no doubt.

"I guess I can't argue with that, but we did take your car."

"God, you're such a redhead." Dawson shook his head. "Technically, it wasn't my car."

"Fine, you win," she relented. "This time."

Tonight, between the sheets, they'd both be victors.

# CHAPTER 8

From the back of her closet, Lacey carefully slipped out the little red dress so the sale tags wouldn't catch on anything and tear the delicate material. She'd purchased it three months ago for her ten-year college reunion. In the dressing room of a boutique shop on Rodeo Drive she'd felt powerful, sexy, and ready to knock her former classmates off their feet. At home, her reflection had told a different story. To attend a party filled with people she hadn't seen since she'd graduated, the dress had suddenly screamed of desperation. For one of Aaron's charity dinners it would shout mistress.

She was Aaron's right hand man, not his arm candy. Her job was to blend in, working behind the scenes so he could shine. But tonight, she needed all eyes on her and off her fake boss. It had nothing to do with wanting to look sexy for Dawson and everything to do with creating speculation about their relationship status to keep the public from noticing anything amiss with the CEO.

Yet when she slid on the dress, the silky fabric morphed into Dawson's hands, sinfully gliding over her curves. A shuddered breath escaped.

A knock sounded, jarring her from the fantasy. Sure, now he was early. If her body tingled from a mere daydream, how would it respond to the dream coming true? To have him touch her in an intimate way, more than the slight contact when she had brushed his hand while passing him his late morning coffee. That innocent exchange altered everything. Was it so innocent? She could have easily placed the mug on his desk. Instead, she'd felt the need to be close to him. To experience the same zing of awareness when he'd grabbed her arm at his bar.

She pressed her cool hands to her blushing cheeks. She opened the door to her modest, two-bedroom, ranch home, prepared to see Aaron's look-a-like, but there was no mistaking the man standing there as anyone but Dawson. Both were confident men, but Dawson radiated sexuality from his eyes to the way he smiled, hell, even the way he stood, slightly forward like he was waiting for a kiss.

"Lacey, if you expect me keep my hands off you, then you've worn the wrong dress."

An electric current shot through her. One would think she'd never been on the other side of a compliment before, but it was the implications of his hands on her and where it would lead to that created the buzz in her blood. Okay, so a small, but deep, part of her craved this exact reaction from him.

What little fabric hugged her body was suddenly too much. With an impeccably cut tuxedo, Dawson was dressed perfectly for the dinner but way overdressed for the thoughts of her smutty mind.

She'd never had these feelings for her real boss. And Aaron would never buy her flowers. "Are those for me?" she asked.

"Oh, yeah," he said, thrusting the bouquet forward like he'd forgotten all about them.

"How did you know sunflowers are my favorite?"

He smiled. "From the screensaver on your laptop."

She blinked. He'd noticed? A guy noticing anything but a beautiful woman, a beer, or a game on TV was hard to come by. Or maybe as a military man he was more aware of his surroundings? Or maybe he was interested in more than a romp between the sheets? She bit her lip.

"Do you want to come in?" To her ears, there was no mistaking the innuendo in her voice.

"Aw, hell. I don't think that's a good idea."

She thought just the opposite. Here he was being responsible, and she was the reckless one. Acting all come hither was totally out of character for her. "I'll just put these in water." After noting the state of her kitchen, she was thankful he hadn't followed. The maid, the one luxury she allowed herself, was due in the morning.

After quickly taking care of the flowers, she locked the door behind her. Dawson waited patiently, leaning against one of the porch columns with his hands in his pockets.

"All ready," she said, suddenly as nervous as if she were on a date with a prince.

Up ahead, a shiny silver chariot awaited. "The Aston Martin?" she asked.

"I feel like James Bond in this get up, so why not? And you, my darling, put all those Bond girls to shame."

*Bond girl?* With their sexist names and disposable nature, she should have been offended, but as Dawson opened the car door and held out his hand to assist her, she felt as beautiful and dangerous as one. After all, she was attending a party with an imposter. It was all rather clandestine, causing excitement to pulse in her veins. Or was it from Dawson's lingering effect on her skin?

Dawson sped along the highway to their destination, driving with an expertise that showed he had no problems handling everything he touched.

"Thinking of buying one for yourself?" She'd hate to see this modest man become jaded and end up losing all his money. Lacey made a note to hook him up with a financial advisor.

"Nah." Dawson shrugged. "Don't get me wrong. I'm having the time of my life driving this fine piece of machinery. But in Alaska, I'll be better off with a truck."

*Alaska.* She'd almost forgotten. When Aaron returned, Dawson would leave for the wilds of the bush, grow back the beard, and trade in the suits for worn jeans. All the more reason not to pursue her wicked train of thought and betray her boss by sleeping with his double. How could she work for Aaron after that? Would she begin to crave his touch, too? Not a chance.

During the drive, she went over some of the names of the attendees, flashing him pictures from her phone during the red traffic lights. Dawson pulled up to the valet and handed off the keys. He frowned as he reached her door, finding she'd had already gotten out.

"What?" she asked.

"Equality is one thing, Lacey, but manners never go out of style."

For fear of being overheard, she didn't tell him that his brother wasn't so much a Neanderthal when it came to social etiquette but more like royalty, expecting everyone to cater to him.

They entered the swanky hotel ballroom. It was already filled with people, and she realized they were the last to arrive.

She felt him stiffen beside her. Did he see someone he knew? Oh no, did he suffer from PTSD? She should have warned him that this was a dinner to raise money for veterans, but she'd wanted to surprise him. With King Enterprises' numerous contacts, she'd already begun the search for Boots. Not wanting to get Dawson's hopes up, she didn't mention it in case the dog couldn't be found.

"What's the matter?" she asked, more concerned with Dawson's well being than the success of tonight's ruse.

"Am I supposed to know all these people?"

"Not all." She put her hand on his bicep and squeezed. "Don't worry, I'll be by your side all night."

"All night?" he whispered.

Oh, dear God, if she was wearing panties they would've dropped to her ankles. "Stop being naughty. Aaron is as straight-laced as a man can be."

Before they joined the throng of guests, Dawson said, "Makes sense that King Enterprises supports the troops, considering they manufacture weapons for the military."

That used to be what Lacey cynically thought, but now she suspected a different motivation for the company's support of the military. And that reason was Dawson. Whatever family feud being fought between them, this was proof there remained something the brothers could hold on to and build upon once Aaron returned. She was sure of it.

* * *

THE EVENING WAS A SUCCESS. If she didn't have time to whisper a name, she'd say, "Mr. King, you remember..."

She admired how easily he adapted, but Dawson really shone when dealing with the wounded vets. Lacey wondered if he bore any scars or if his were the kind that left an emotional mark.

As the party waned, Lacey sat at an empty table and slipped off the literal killer heels strangling her feet. "Thank goodness there's no dancing," she said.

Placing his hands on her shoulders, Dawson bent and whispered in her ear before taking the seat next to her. "I don't know, it would've been a reason to hold you in my arms."

Her mouth went dry. After snagging a glass of champagne from a passing waiter, she downed the contents, which instead of providing relief, created bubbles of mayhem. Underneath the table, Dawson lifted her foot onto his lap, and with hands that should be memorialized in marble, massaged. The pain blending with pleasure was utterly exquisite. Oh, dear God, she was going to come. She had to fight closing her eyes as tingles drew up.

"Ready to call it a night?" he asked, his voice husky like he'd been on the receiving end of the massage.

She replaced one foot for the other. "Almost."

He laughed. "I think I've made a huge mistake."

"Huge." That wasn't the only thing that was huge. She tried to maneuver her foot so she could feel the full length of him, but he pinched her pinky toe. She stopped so he could continue to work his magic.

"Okay. I'm ready."

"I'm not. We'll have to wait a moment." Dawson opened a bottle of water and took a long drink.

"Don't tell me you have a foot fetish."

"No, I have a fetish for the way your eyes fluttered and the way you whimpered for me."

"I did not whimper," she insisted as she slipped her shoes on.

A mix of anticipation and dread warred within her. Foot massage aside, this wasn't a date, she reminder herself for the tenth time tonight. But she wanted it to be.

His silence on the car ride only made it worse. So she got back to business and broke the quiet by citing him a to-do-list for tomorrow.

When Dawson pulled up to the curb, he turned off the car and reached for the driver's side door handle.

"You don't have to walk me to the door."

"If it makes you feel better, consider it a safety issue."

And he did make her feel safe as they walked the path to her house in silence, the June full moon lighting the way. Upon reaching the porch, she searched her bag for the keys.

"Can I kiss you, Lacey?"

He was asking permission? Unable to form a yes, she answered with a slight nod.

He put a finger underneath her chin to tilt her head and gazed intently into her eyes "Say it," he demanded, like his life depended on it.

If she didn't, she knew she'd regret it for the rest of hers. "Yes," she half said, half whimpered.

His eyes didn't gleam with victory but with desire as he placed his lips upon hers. As gentle as a warm summer breeze, his kiss was tailored to make a woman sigh, to stir buried passions. He whetted her appetite when she hadn't even known she was starving. And when he pulled away, she stood frozen outwardly, but inside, the wanting grew and grew.

Finally, she opened her eyes. His heated gaze was anything but tender.

"I expected a rough kiss," she whispered, though she hadn't meant to.

"I didn't want to scare you." His voice was guttural, a contrast to the way he stroked her cheek.

"I'm not scared," she said, regaining her voice.

"No? But now I am."

Of what? That he might break her? Or that she might break him? At the moment, the answer didn't matter. All that did was for their lips to join again. And if he could ask for a kiss, then so could she. He said he was all about equality.

"Can I kiss you?" she braved, feeling empowered by her question but also the worry of his rejection.

"I'm all yours."

His response thrilled her. "All mine?" she asked, sliding her hands along the lapels of his tux and then a slight tug as a signal for Dawson to bend his head so she could capture his lips. Now it was her turn. She was as fierce as he'd been gentle, showing him what she craved. What she needed.

Dawson was a fast learner, and he took control of the kiss, and of her. He hauled her body up against him, one hand grabbed her ass cheek, and the other delved into her hair.

*Yes. This.*

In one breath, she was a conqueror, and then the very next, a slave. Equality was a good thing outside of the bedroom, but behind closed doors—or in this case, outside the front door of her house—the raw power of Dawson's response was oh-so-welcomed.

Dawson was all hers and she all his. Equal.

# CHAPTER 9

*T*he wildcat in his arms stole his breath and rewarded with him life, all in one soul-changing kiss. Dawson had expected the redhead to have heat, but oh, unholy hell, nothing could have prepared him for the firestorm she ignited.

Running a hand along her curves, he found enough of the silky fabric to gather in his fist. Not wanting to be a brute, he denied himself the pleasure of ripping it from her body so he could feel her skin, which he'd bet his payday was just as sleek.

She tasted of champagne and chocolate. Heady and sweet. The combination left him reeling in an abyss of need. He desired her more than anything he'd ever wanted before. More than money. More than home. More than a relationship with his father. Or his brother.

*Aaron. Hell.*

He didn't give a shit about his twin's warning to

stay away from his assistant. But was Lacey kissing Dawson and thinking of Aaron? *Fuck that.*

That was never part of the fantasy.

Breaking away, he ended what she had started. He watched as she caught her breath, trying to read her mind, her emotions. Impossible, until she opened her eyes. Confused. Dazed. Unfilled.

He wished he could replace the look with one of satisfaction. To leave her sated.

That would be selfish though. The resulting aftermath of one night of passion between them would echo into her future. Messy. Complicated. Things he strove to avoid.

"Goodnight, Lacey."

"What's wrong?"

Unwilling to admit he feared she desired Aaron over him, he said. "You're a little tipsy."

Hurt flashed in her eyes, but then the blaze lit, and he knew he was about to get his ass handed to him.

"I must be, if I was kissing you." She turned away and stabbed at the keyhole multiple times, like she was pretending it was his heart.

"Let me."

"I can unlock it myself," she snapped. This time the key slipped in. "And you know what, I can walk myself from the car to my house." She turned the key and pushed. "Oh, and look, I can open doors all by myself."

Her redheaded fury was in full glory. Damn, if he didn't want to see if he could kiss it away. Instead, he stood there and took the full brunt of her anger because he deserved it.

She stepped in, and without looking back, slammed the door in his face.

Right now, she hated him. In the morning, she'd thank him for it.

It was almost the hardest thing he ever had to do. Killing men had a way of putting things in perspective. But saving Lacey from herself—yeah, that was right up there.

When he drove up the driveway of his brother's mansion, he cursed himself for being a gentleman. *Ha! Starting to believe your own bullshit, Dawson?*

He was no gentleman, only a man, who, upon finding out he still had a heart, was afraid of losing it, and this time for good.

The butler greeted him at the door. "How was your night, Mr. King?"

Why was he calling him Mr. King? There was no one around to overhear. "It went well."

With a stern fatherly expression he asked, "And Miss Lacey?"

Dawson was thankful to admit, "Her virtue is intact."

With a slight tilt of the head, Edward said, "What a shame."

"So she and—"

"Never."

Relief flooded through him. "I wonder how he's doing."

"I do, too. Glad to hear that you are." Edward lingered, looking over his shoulder like he was expecting someone to appear.

"What's the matter, Edward?"

"Uh. How do I put this?" The butler wrung his hands. "Your Monday night guest is the game room."

"Guest?" asked Dawson, peering down the hall then back at Edward. He whispered, "Paid guest?"

Edward shrugged. "Not in the way you think."

Well, that was cryptic. Why hadn't Aaron canceled? In the rush to get to rehab, had he forgotten? Dawson was sure Lacey didn't have this appointment on her boss' schedule.

"What am I supposed to do with her?" Dawson asked.

"Get rid of her."

"Isn't that your job, Edward?"

"How does your generation say it?" He tapped his chin. "Oh, yes, it's complicated. When you meet Sophia, you'll understand."

Dawson trudged down the hall. Was Sophia a high-priced call girl? Was the game room more than just air hockey and pinball?

Not knowing what to expect, he schooled his face into a mask of stone. Dawson assumed his billionaire brother would have a hot young blond chick at his disposal, but the perfectly coifed woman who posed by the eight-foot pool table had to be pushing fifty. Tall, full-figured, and brunette, she wore a mid-thigh, tight white skirt, a black blouse with a red lace bra performing a peek-a-boo with the buttons.

"Aaron! Finally." She approached him with swaying hips that should hypnotize a man. But not Dawson. His dick didn't even so much as twinge. Faithful like a dog to its owner, it apparently already belonged to Lacey.

"The usual?" She went for his belt.

And Lacey thought her boss was straight-laced? He gently swept Sophia's hand aside. "Not tonight."

"Too bad. I thought you might change your mind."

So Aaron had canceled. Dawson figured he'd keep it short and simple. If his brother had an ongoing relationship with this woman, there would be little chance of fooling her. "No."

Sophia tilted her head. "You look different."

*Crap.* "I'm tired."

Sophia shook her head. "No, you look the opposite of tired. Your face is flushed, and your eyes are actually twinkling with a different shade of blue." Then she gave a fake laugh. "Oh God, don't tell me the mighty Aaron King has fallen in love?"

Never. But he could see how a guy could fall down the rabbit hole by losing himself in Lacey's arms.

"Nothing so drastic. I'll call you when I'm ready resume our arrangement."

She reached into her purse and pulled out a bag of prescription bottles. "I'm sure you're getting low."

She was Aaron's lover and drug supplier?

Upon his brother's return, would Aaron relapse and call Sophia for a fix? Probably. Right now, Dawson was in a position to help or at least block his brother's access to his source. But once the mission was complete, he wasn't coming back to help. No matter what. No matter how much money Aaron promised.

"On second thought, Sophia. There's no sense in

dragging this out. I'm clean. As part of that, I have to cut ties with you."

"Clean and sober? Ah, so that's why you look different." She threw the hoard of pills back in her purse. "Well, I'm not going to beg for one more lay for old times' sake. Don't call when you need a fix—and that includes my tight little pussy that you're just as addicted to." With a flip of her hair, she said, "I'll see myself out."

Dawson expelled a breath when he heard a front door slam for the second time tonight. That was a first for him. At least this one wasn't in his face. Then he heard breaking glass.

He ran to the entryway. The gap in the living room window was the size of the rock on the floor. The moonlight flickered off the glass strewn about the room. The butler appeared with a broom.

"That went well," stated Edward.

Dawson couldn't tell if he was serious or sarcastic.

"It could have been your head," Edward continued.

His brother owed him for burning that toxic bridge. Whatever the agreement between Aaron and Sophia entailed, it was clear his brother had no romantic interest in his executive assistant, clearing the path for Dawson to pursue her. And if Lacey secretly carried a torch for his brother, Dawson would extinguish it and replace it with a raging inferno that burned only for him.

Assuming she wasn't still pissed at him.

# CHAPTER 10

*O*n the ride up the elevator the next morning, Lacey practiced her speech out loud.

"About what happened…thank you for saving me from myself. I was indeed a bit tipsy." *No. No.* Such a lie. She hadn't been inebriated at all, at least not from the champagne.

"Let's forget about it and move on." Only she'd remember that kiss forever. Hold it up as *THE* kiss. The one she'd compare all others to. The one she'd reminisce about on her deathbed.

"You kissed me first." There, that sounded more like her, but it was childish, and Dawson made her feel like a woman. For the last five years, she'd worked herself to the top of King Enterprises at the expense of having any sexual relationships. She hadn't even missed it—until last night.

If he were a true gentleman, he'd apologize, or at

the very least not bring it up at all. That's it! She'd pretend like nothing happened.

She took a detour to the employee breakroom to delay the inevitable awkward confrontation. While waiting for the coffee to brew, she paced the floor as she assessed her options yet again. She concluded that silence wasn't one of them. It would drive her crazy wondering what Dawson was thinking, waiting for him to address the elephant in the room. She'd never been one to sit back and let things happen.

After taking a sip of coffee, she poured a cup for Dawson as a peace offering. As a 'no biggie, your rejection had no effect on my confidence as a woman—or on my heart'. Geez, she was expecting a lot from a cup of coffee.

Soon the employees would be filtering in, so she smoothed her knee-length black skirt, made sure the buttons on her light gray blouse were intact, and checked the mirror, reapplying a stroke of lipstick and fluffing her hair. The color matched the current blush in her cheeks.

*Suck it up, buttercup.* She took a deep breath, and then headed for the reckoning.

Juggling the handles of the mugs in one hand, she opened the door to the CEO's office and kicked it closed.

"Good morning, Lacey."

For all her practice, the words stalled in her throat. And how was it a good morning? Looking like a sharp-dressed man, Dawson must have slept like a baby while she tossed and turned, replaying the night over and over again.

He took the mugs from her hand and placed them on the desk. "Lacey, I apologize—"

"No need," she cut him off, looking away. "You were totally right to—"

"No, I was dead wrong."

Her gaze met his. His fevered eyes fanned the embers stoking in her blood. "You were?"

He stepped closer, invading her personal space like a wolf sniffing out his prey. "Yes. I never should have stopped."

He pulled her into his arms. This time, there was no asking for permission. No softness or probing. Just a full-on lips to lips, picking up right where they left off.

It wasn't a kiss meant for the light of day, as the sun rose over the city. It was kiss meant for the shadows or a midnight rendezvous.

Dawson slipped his hand underneath her blouse, and she, in turn, slid her hands inside his suit jacket exploring the male power of his body.

His hand drew up to push aside the cup of her bra. He closed his fingers around her naked breast, sending a jolt of sexual awareness through her.

The sofa beckoned. So did the conference room table. Up against the floor-to-ceiling windows. Every available square inch of the office suddenly became a possibility.

He tugged up her skirt, grabbed her ass, and then lifted her against the hard length of him. Lacey wanted him buried deep inside. Now.

She broke the kiss. "Condom?"

"Fuck." He leaned his forehead against hers. The sound of their harsh breaths only created more tension, more heat between them. "Would it be sexual harassment to ask my executive assistant to run out to buy some?"

"Yes! Well, normally it would."

They both burst out laughing, expending pent-up frustration from going lighting speed to a dead stop.

"Guess we need to be adults."

"Adulting sucks," said Dawson.

"As opposed to being horny teenagers?" Lacey pushed down her skirt and smoothed out the wrinkles.

"I'm no fumbling teenage boy." His gaze left her exposed breast and rose to her eyes. "I don't want to merely fuck you, Lacey."

"Oh—" The door opened. "Dottie!"

"Oh, sorry. Was I interrupting something?"

"I can explain." Dawson stood in front of Lacey as she adjusted her clothes.

Dottie sighed. "Don't worry. Your secret is safe with me, just as your father's were."

"I'm nothing like my father."

The ferociousness in Dawson's voice shocked Lacey. She peered around his body to see how the secretary was reacting.

Dottie tapped her foot. "Don't use that tone with me, young man."

Finished with shifting her bra back into place, Lacey left the protection of Dawson's back and bravely faced Dottie. Yesterday's conversation in the breakroom haunted her. If word spread to the other employees, she'd lose the respect she'd earned. "It was mistake. We were arguing and then we were kissing. That's it. It won't happen again."

Dottie took her hand and patted it. "Yes, it will, dear. You wouldn't be the first to fall for the charms of one of the King men."

What did that mean? Had Dottie had an affair with Aaron's father? Grandfather? She'd just celebrated her fortieth anniversary with the company, so it could be possible.

"Next time, lock the door. I may have changed your diapers, Aaron, but you're too old for me to see you in your birthday suit." Dottie bustled out, closing the door with a thud.

Lacey bridged her fingers across her forehead and faced a stunned Dawson. "What are we going to do?"

"She changed Aaron's diapers?"

She grabbed his biceps in a panic, though she wasn't that upset not to appreciate the size and strength of his arms. "Focus," she said for the both of them. "What if she changes her mind and tells your father?"

His brow furrowed. "I'll tell him to mind his own damn business."

"You don't understand. Aaron would never say anything remotely like that. He calls him 'sir!'"

"Sir?" Dawson shook his head. "Sweet Jesus. Unbelievable. And I thought it was bad I had to call my mother by her first name since I was eight."

She filed that bit of information away. The question of the nature of the King family dynamics stayed at the tip of her tongue, but Lacey's main concern for the moment, as much as she hated to admit it, was for herself. "What about my professional reputation? What will the other employees think if I get promoted to VP?"

"If they're honest, they'll know you worked your ass off for it."

Lacey snorted. "Worked my ass off in bed, you mean."

The corner of his lips quirked into a half-smile. "Stop talking dirty to me."

She took a deep breath to keep her temper under control. Dawson must have noticed because he immediately backtracked.

"Look, Lacey, let's cross that bridge when we come to it. Dottie said our secret is safe, and I believe her." He handed her cup to her while taking a sip from his own. "She didn't last in this company by divulging company or personal secrets."

"True," she said, slightly mollified by what he said and by the scent of his musky cologne. Definitely not a scent Aaron would choose.

"Now, what's on the agenda today?"

She gazed into the caramel-colored liquid in her mug, hoping to see the future like a fortune-telling gypsy reading coffee grounds. An image of her as VP materialized, but she still wasn't happy. It didn't make sense. VP was her goal. Her dream.

She squared her shoulders. "Okay, there's a meeting with marketing. And then we need to start prepping for next week's meeting with Yuen Corporation."

"Any rule in the employee handbook that says we can't work from home?"

She raised a brow. "Work?"

"Yeah." He stalked closer, like it was impossible for him to keep his distance from her. "In fact, I have feeling there will be overtime involved. Is that a problem?"

As if she didn't constantly toil around the clock for one big fat salary, but working extra hours with Dawson would be far more pleasurable than money. At least at home there'd be no prying eyes. She slipped her hands up his shirtfront and straightened his tie.

"Well, you are the boss."

# CHAPTER 11

*E*ven in mid-afternoon, the L.A. traffic was horrendous. Dawson felt the familiar squeezing inside his chest as the crush of the surrounding cars suffocated him. His heart raced along with his mind while everything around him grounded to a halt. He tugged off his tie, and then shrugged out of his suit jacket.

He hadn't had a full-on anxiety attack in months. Alaska had turned out to be the perfect place to recover and relearn to live in the real world. Except for the community of other veterans, there was little reminder of the scorching Afghanistan days or the endless desert terrain.

Alaska, refreshingly cold with deep forests of greenery and the white frozen tundra, was the balm his soul needed. He'd trade the sand for snow for all of eternity.

Sometimes, Dawson was guilt-ridden about not reenlisting, but he knew he'd actually be guilty if he had stayed on. If one of his internal battles hit during physical combat with the enemy and led to one his brothers in arms' death, he wouldn't have been able to live with himself.

And at other times, he felt like a chicken shit. A coward. And that was hard to live with, too.

He inhaled a deep breath and let it go. He'd learned work-a-rounds from the VA, like grounding exercises that kept the anxiety at bay.

*Step One. Look around. Find five things you see.*

Out loud he said, "Cars. Trucks. Windshield. Steering Wheel. Lacey's smile." Inside his mind didn't count though, so he added, "My hands."

*Step Two. Name four things you can touch.*

He grazed his fingers along the dashboard, the stick shift, the rearview mirror, and the place on his skin where Lacey had brushed her fingers, causing goose-bumps to prick along his forearm.

*Step Three. Name three things you hear.*

Blaring horns, the sound of his blood rushing through his body—no don't think about that. Skip to the next one…

*Step Four. Name two things you can smell.*

Exhaust. Gunfire—no—this wasn't helping. Fuck.

*Step Five. Name one thing you can taste.*

That one was easy. And the one Dawson should focus on. Meditate on. The honeyed flavor of Lacey's lips still lingered upon his memory.

But this exercise wasn't supposed to be built on memories, it was supposed to ground him in the here and now. But Lacey was his now. Keeping his mind on what awaited him was the remedy he needed.

After a boring, mind-numbing meeting with the marketing department, Dawson had raced to a local drugstore to purchase a box of condoms and a bottle of Rosè, and then bee-lined for Lacey's house. They'd mutually agreed to her turf to prevent Edward from finding out. And Dawson really didn't need to be reminded of his brother while making love to Lacey or for her to have any thoughts of Aaron.

The traffic crawled another mile. The engine of the Jaguar revved, clearly just as antsy as Dawson was.

Finally, he pulled up to the front of Lacey's house and turned off the ignition. It took several minutes to shake off the remnants of his anxiety, which lingered like a sun shower. Today, though, Lacey would be his rainbow.

Instead of thinking it was a mistake to mix business with pleasure, she was the one thing he was sure of.

So why did he have to summon up the courage to leave the car, especially when, minutes ago, it had felt like a prison? Grabbing the wine and the condoms, he cursed himself for not taking the time to buy flowers, too. She deserved flowers.

Faltering in his step, he stopped three quarters of the way up the pathway. What was he doing? Lacey deserved a man who could give her everything. At the very least, a woman needed a man who didn't crumble and a man who could stick around. He was neither of those.

He was still standing frozen in indecision when the door whipped open.

"You're here." She look surprised, almost like she'd expected him to change his mind and cut bait. She still wore the sexy pencil skirt and blouse.

He strode up the rest of the way. "I hit traffic." He thrust the wine into her hands, and before he could stop himself, the condoms, too.

Lacey blinked. "Oh."

Standing inside the entryway, he felt like a lout. *Come on, Dawson, you got better moves than that.*

He followed her into the farmhouse kitchen. The décor of red and white-checkered curtains trimmed with roosters, a sign that said 'Morning Y'all', and an old-fashioned apron hung from the doorknob surprised him. An image of Lacey wearing it with nothing underneath rose in his mind. That wasn't the only thing that rose.

After sneaking a peek at her salary today, he was surprised she lived in a modest neighborhood. Aaron paid her well, but she lived below her means. Still, he preferred this quirky feminine décor to his brother's opulent interior design. Aaron had a house, and Lacey had a home.

Lacey placed the wine in the 1950's retro fridge. He guessed they were skipping the alcohol for now.

"Nice place," he said.

Still holding the condoms with one hand, she curled

her fingers around his belt then tugged him closer. "Wanna see the bedroom?"

"Damn, woman." He hauled her into a kiss, loving how she could go from zero to a hundred on a dime.

All thoughts of work and the outside world faded.

Lacey guided him to her room. His gaze was drawn to the queen-sized bed with oversized, cream and pink flowered pillows. Underneath the businesswoman persona, she was a gypsy at heart.

Sheer white curtains did nothing to block the sun, its rays pouring onto the bed like their personal spotlight. Good, he wanted to see her in all her naked splendor.

With her fingers still clutching his belt, she led him to the foot of the bed, pushed him to a sitting position, and tossed the box of condoms onto the puffy, white silk comforter. Then she stood an arm's length away.

She unbuttoned her blouse to reveal a blush-colored bra that barely hid the rosy tips of her breasts. His mouth watered to the point where he thought he'd drool, so he swallowed hard. She shimmied out of her skirt. He rubbed his jaw to prevent his mouth from dropping open at the site of her matching undies, which were so flimsy he could and *would* rip them off with one firm tug. If he wasn't already sitting, he had have fallen to his knees.

The businesswoman with a gypsy heart wearing the lingerie of a siren called to him like Odysseus lost at sea.

"Jesus, Lacey, you were wearing that underneath your clothes all morning?"

She played a finger along the banded lace of the panties. "Yes."

Dawson worked at the buttons of his shirt. "It's a good thing I didn't know about it."

"Or you would've what?" She took a step toward him.

Though she was tantalizingly close enough for him to reach out and capture her, he was patient. "Or we never would have made it out of the office," he growled, removing his shirt, then stood to shed his pants.

Lacey pushed him again to sit and then straddled his lap. Already hard from her strip tease, the feel of her pussy rubbing against his cock eased the ache and created a raging need all at the same torturous time.

Her sweet lips descended upon his. She kissed him into a frenzied beast until he finally had enough. Flipping her onto her back, he took control.

Still, Dawson showed his saintly patience by trailing kisses down her neck, to her collarbone. His tongue played along the soft swell of her breast. Then he bit the edges of her bra cups like the wolf and tugged, so he could feast on her nipples.

"Dawson." Her voice, like an angel's whisper to his ears, echoed in his empty soul. Her touch, like feathered wings, left a path of goose bumps. The opium scent of her though was like sin, enveloping him in an embrace of lust.

Her hands became more insistent. "Lower."

Obeying, Dawson dragged his hands along the sides of her curves while raining tiny kisses and licks down until he reached her pussy. With a growl, her undies received the same treatment as her bra had.

"Please," she moaned, but she wasn't shy, spreading her legs, allowing him full access to her pussy.

"You're as bossy in the bedroom as you are out of it."

"I said, please."

Dawson chuckled, his mouth already tasting the sweet pink satin of her sex. The vibration caused Lacey to giggle, but it quickly turned to breathless moans as he worshipped her body. Bringing her to the edge of Nirvana, he denied her entry by easing the pressure of his tongue. He devoted himself to her pleasure and hoped his reward would be salvation in her arms.

"Dawson," she pleaded.

Her thighs clenched his head like a vise, and he knew there was no bringing her back from the brink this time, so he stiffened his tongue and flicked again and again.

"Dawson!"

No longer a plea, but not a scream either—more like a gasp of awakening. Her body shuddered, and his cock throbbed in anticipation of getting in the game. His mouth was merely the foreplay to the big show.

He rose to his knees to watch the last of the orgasm ripping through her. Mesmerized by the sight, he fumbled for the box of condoms without looking away. Her eyes opened as he sheathed his cock. The green of her irises were smoky like a genie rising out of her bottle. Would she grant him three wishes? He had only one.

"Lacey?"

A soft sexy smile appeared on her lips.

Dawson slid into her tight wet heat, and instead of the salvation he sought, he tumbled into a silky abyss of rapture. Lost in his need for her, he found a reason for his heart to beat.

# CHAPTER 12

*D*awson's heated breath had lit sparks along her skin. And now his wet kiss as he entered her only added fuel to the fire. She needed to come, to douse the flames consuming her. Only his sweet, long, easy strokes tortured instead of eased. Desperate for short hard pumps, she tried to control the pace by moving her hips. She was so ready, so close.

"Tell me what you want, Lacey," he ordered in a husky whisper. His teeth grazed her neck. "I'll do anything for you."

Dare she say it? Dare she not? "Fuck me, Dawson."

"Like this?"

The rapid pace he set matched the beat of her heart.

"Yes...no...harder."

And now the pounding of his body against hers matched the blood pulsing through her.

Her breath quickened. Short gasps, building to one

long gulp for air before going under, until she unleashed the exhale into a primal scream of release of, "Yes!"

Pleasure ripped through her body in a thunderous wave, but its wake left her aching for more. More of what she couldn't pinpoint.

Then Dawson wrapped her up in his arms. "Anything," he murmured.

*Yes, this is what I want more of.*

She settled into his embrace, sated and happy. It was a fleeting feeling, she knew. The pleasure would fade, and with it, the real world would unravel the web of lies she was weaving.

Lies of a future with Dawson.

Perhaps when Aaron returned he'd be so grateful he'd ask Dawson to join the business. But deep down, she knew Dawson wasn't the corporate type, or even the LA type. He'd suffocate here. The crowds. The wealth. The heat. In the moments when no one was looking and his guard was down, she could see how he itched to be back home.

He said he'd do anything for her, but would that including staying in LA.? It wouldn't be fair to ask him to.

But was it fair that every time she would sit across from Aaron, she'd be reminded of Dawson? Of this perfect moment?

She could move to Alaska.

*Oh hell, no! Since when did you turn into your mother?*

If she repeated history, falling for and then

following the bad boy, she had only herself to blame. Only Dawson wasn't such a bad boy, was he? He was helping out his brother even though outwardly he showed only resentment toward Aaron. And he was using some of the money to find his dog. Yes, she was truly a master weaver of lies.

She'd probably just forgotten how good sex was. It was always that amazing. Right? Well there was only one way to find out.

Lacey turned around his arms and maneuvered him onto his back. His sexy, sleepy half-smile woke into a full blown one.

She straddled his thighs and fisted his semi, which quickly turned to iron in her hand. Ah, so much better than a man turning to putty in her hands. At first, she leisurely petted his cock.

Dawson gritted his teeth. "Such sweet torture," he said.

She showed him mercy. The motion of her hand gave a whole new meaning to pumping iron.

"Damn, woman." Dawson tossed her a condom. "Come on, Lacey. I'm dying to feel your heat again."

Once again, she straddled him, this time sliding her wet, aching pussy onto his cock. At first, she rocked her hips, clutching him inside her.

"Tell me want you want." She clawed a hand down his chest to his abs. "I'll do anything for you."

The blue of his eyes heated. "I want you to use me. Use my cock for your own pleasure."

Lacey wasn't shy. She rode him like a boss.

The buildup was exquisite. The release so intense it

almost hurt. And she knew, in that moment, that it was more than just sex.

Yes, Dawson's body was hotter than hell. Yes, his cock was big. And God, yes, he knew how to use it. But as she drifted down, their gazes connected, and their heavy breaths mingled. A tightrope of unsaid words stretched between them. Dare she walk across it and reveal her feelings?

In her experience, it would send a man running. And Dawson would run back all the way back to Alaska. Then how would she explain her failure to Aaron?

So she looked away and rolled off him to head to the bathroom without saying what was in her heart.

* * *

LATER THAT NIGHT, they sat at her dining room table going over the Yuen file. Empty Chinese food cartons lay strewn about with the paperwork. Lacey had slid on a sensible pair of pajama bottoms and a matching T-shirt while a shirtless Dawson only wore pants.

She kept peeking over the screen of her laptop, remembering how she used his muscular chest as an anchor to steady more than her body. His sculpted biceps could take control of her or hold her with such gentleness her heart melted. The table hid his abs, so she lifted herself an inch or two off her seat. Damn, she wasn't getting a whole lot of work done.

"Lacey?"

She dropped her butt and gaze before he caught her ogling. "Hmm..."

"Did you meet Aaron in Harvard?"

She stopped typing and looked up. "You looked at my personnel record?"

Dawson spun Aaron's laptop around. "Yeah."

Her file was up on the screen, along with an unflattering employee security photo. "How? Even Aaron doesn't have direct access to the Human Resources."

"King Enterprises' firewall is a joke. I wouldn't be surprised if China hasn't already hacked it and stolen company secrets."

Dawson rubbed the stubble on his jaw. She blushed, feeling the chafe on her inner thighs. Then berated herself for not thinking of her employer first. Had security been breached? Instead of checking off items on the agenda, her to-do-list grew. The added responsibility of cyber-security weighed heavily upon her.

"Which brings me to why is Aaron doing business with the Chinese?"

She blinked from the abrupt change of conversation. "It's a Chinese company, not the government."

"Same difference."

That was an odd comment. "What exactly was your specialty in the Army?"

"Jack of all trades."

Lacey smiled. "Master of none?"

"You're well aware of what I'm a master in."

She rose from the chair and rounded the table. "It seems I have developed short-term memory loss."

Sitting on his lap, she flashed her best come-hither look. "Perhaps I need a reminder."

"Impressive evasive tactics, Lacey Brooks."

"What?" she asked innocently.

"Distracting me with sex."

"Apparently not impressive enough," she sulked.

His hand slid between her thighs. "Oh, I'd say they are."

She wiggled in his lap and received an answering salute from his cock.

"But I'm a patient man." He smiled.

And she was an impatient woman who could only think about his lips on hers.

"We were in the same study group."

"That's it? You are very loyal to him."

"You sound jealous."

"Maybe I am." He shrugged, not committing to either a yes or a no.

She guessed it was a yes. But was he jealous merely because Aaron had money and privilege? Or did it go deeper than that? She'd like to think so.

"Don't be. It's not like that. Never was. You see I was at the top of all my classes. Aaron defended me when some students accused me of having affairs with the professors in exchange for better grades. Of course, it couldn't be because I was smarter than them or worked twice as hard as them. As if the only way a woman could beat them out was by fucking her way to the top."

"I guess my brother isn't a total shit."

"No, and I never forgot his support. When he took

over as CEO, he asked me to help him. I really wasn't interested in living in L.A., but my college loans loomed, and he made me an offer I couldn't refuse."

"I know the feeling."

They shared a smile. She placed her hand on his heart, hoping one day they could share that, too.

CHAPTER 13

*a* week of long days pouring over spreadsheets and short nights between the sheets flew by. Dawson and Lacey held court with the Yuen executives at the conference table in his office. *His?* How easily he'd slipped into the role of CEO and into his brother's life, a life that should have been his, too.

Still, he missed his bar, even the patrons, who provided enough antics to keep it amusing. Mostly, he worried about the homeless vets who washed up and grabbed a meal before hitting the streets. Any one of them could've been him. All of them his brothers in arms.

While Lacey expertly handled the negotiations for the sale of the King Enterprises' Outdoor Gear Division, Dawson remained silent as he observed Mr. Yuen and his two associates.

Bred to believe the Chinese were the enemy, it

would be a test of his acting skills to get through this meeting.

After her presentation was complete, the three men spoke between themselves in their native language. Dawson understood every word, but kept his mask of stone in place. He had learned Farsi and Arabic for the Army, French for the ladies, and Mandarin for the challenge.

"We are prepared to offer you five hundred million dollars," said one of the associates.

The amount was as Lacey predicted. Dawson was to counter with six hundred million, and then they would come back with five hundred and fifty, and everybody walked away happy. But based on the conversation, he knew something Lacey didn't. Until now, she'd been the one schooling him. He jumped at the opportunity to show off what he learned.

"Six hundred million, not a penny less," he demanded.

His gaze never wavered from Yuen's. Lacey was probably shooting daggers at him anyway.

A quick flurry of foreign words between the three ensued.

Yuen snapped up a hand. *"Gou."* *Enough.*

"Deal." Yuen extended his hand, and Dawson shook it.

"Wonderful," said Lacey.

Her tone was pleasant enough, but Dawson detected something off in her fake smile.

"I'm emailing our law department with the final

number, and they'll walk over the contract," she continued

*Holy. Shit.* He'd just increased King Enterprises' coffers by fifty million dollars. More importantly, the Chinese company hadn't gotten one over on him or on the family, and the deal would set the tone for future negotiations. Though he didn't give a damn about King Enterprises, stupid pride swelled in his chest. In less than thirty minutes, he'd more than made back the money Aaron was giving him.

With the contracts signed and good-bye pleasantries exchanged, Dawson escorted Mr. Yuen and his associates to the door.

When he turned, he could see Lacey mentally counting to ten as she stood by his desk. He smiled. Really, what could she say?

"What the hell just happened?"

He walked over to where she stood by his desk. "You were spectacular."

"I know I was." She fisted her hands on her hips in that cute way of hers. "But then you almost blew the deal with your bravado."

"It wasn't bravado. It's knowing your enemy."

"The enemy?"

"Six is lucky to the Chinese...and I speak Mandarin."

"Seriously?"

"*Wo ai ni.*" So much easier to say *I love you* in a foreign language.

Lacey laughed. "You sound ridiculous. What does it mean?"

She hadn't known what he said, but it still stung that she wasn't impressed with his linguistic skills. "Let's fuck."

"How romantic." She rolled her eyes. Then she jabbed a finger to his chest. "No more going off-script. Remember, I'm the boss of you."

"Miss Brooks, that is no way to talk to my son."

With his back to the door, Dawson had time to school his features and to calm his erratic heartbeat. Lacey wasn't so lucky. Her green eyes widened with fear.

Straightening his tie, he prepared himself to face his father. Before turning, he winked at Lacey and mouthed, "I got this."

"Good Afternoon, sir." He stalled for a moment, waiting, hoping for the man who had part in Dawson's creation to notice some difference from his brother. *To notice him.*

Dressed in a gray pinstriped suit, Aaron Sr. didn't look like a man who was retired. Their father had aged well. A hint of gray touched his temples, and a few deep lines creased his forehead, but he wasn't the towering figure Dawson remembered from his first and only meeting when he was twelve. Emboldened by this, he would not cower in front of him even if Lacey had said Aaron would.

"Miss Brooks is doing what I pay her to do."

"Bitch at you?"

Dawson fisted his hands. "You will apologize to Miss Brooks."

"It's okay," said Lacey.

"No, it is not," Dawson said to Lacey, then turned back to his father and added, "Or would you like Miss Books to file a costly lawsuit?"

A muscle twitched in his father's cheek. "Forgive me, Miss Brooks." He shrugged. "Jet lag," he added, as if it excused his bad manners.

"Of course, Mr. King."

She barely got the words out, and he'd already dismissed her, turning back to his son. "Heard you almost blew the China deal."

Had he spoken with Mr. Yuen has they left? "I made the company an extra fifty million."

"Chump change. If you had lost that deal—

"But I didn't. A simple 'good job' would do."

"I will, when you do."

He knew his father was a prick, but for fuck's sake, what was his problem? Dawson couldn't imagine growing up under his thumb. He almost felt sorry for Aaron. Almost.

"Miss Brooks, leave us. I have business to discuss with my son."

"She stays," demanded Dawson. "She knows the company inside out." And while he didn't want his father getting his own way, Dawson needed Lacey beside him, not only to direct him, but for moral support.

"This is family business."

Lacey scooped up her laptop. Looking down, she would not meet his eyes. "Mr. King." Then nodded to his father. "Mr. King."

He hated seeing her this way. Unsure. Terrified. She

knew her shit while his father treated her like crap. When Aaron returned, Dawson was going to have a long hard talk with him about the company's treatment of Lacey.

His gaze fell to the hypnotic sway of her hips. The thud of the door closing broke the trance. Then, taking the position of power behind the desk, he parked himself on the throne of King Enterprises like nothing in the world was wrong.

"We have a problem," his father said as he strode to the bank of windows. "Your brother's gone missing."

As the former CEO continued to gaze out at the skyline, it allowed Dawson a moment to wipe the surprise off his face and swallow before replying.

"Missing?" He picked up a pen and twirled it in his hand the way Aaron did when he was bored, the way Lacey had taught him to do.

"The bar is closed for renovation, but there's no sign of construction. No sign of him."

Worry creased his father's brow. What did he care? It was much too late for any hope of reconciliation. "He's probably on vacation."

"No, something is wrong."

*Yeah, with your other son.*

"Twenty-two vets commit suicide every day."

"I can assure you my brother would never commit suicide." Not now anyway. A year ago, well... "Your spare heir is probably off in the bush fishing."

"How can you be so sure?" His father finally looked him in the eye.

"He's my twin. I would know." What a crock of shit.

If it were true, then he'd know how Aaron was doing in rehab. Hell, Dawson would've known his brother was addicted to pain killers.

His father nodded thoughtfully, like it eased his mind, though that was the last thing Dawson was going for. But if it kept King from speculating on the whereabouts of his long lost son, then so be it.

"So the gold digger finally has her hooks in you?"

"Who are you talking about?"

"*Miss* Brooks."

Had Dottie said something? Or was it just obvious by the way he looked at Lacey? Dawson played the role of Aaron King brilliantly but was lousy when it came to masking his feelings for Lacey. She was far from the gold digger his father accused her of being. She was the gold behind the company. King Enterprises would be lost without her. *I would be lost without her.* "Miss Brooks is none of your concern."

"Don't speak to me that way."

"I'll do what I damn well please."

"Just remember who made this company."

"Yes, Grandfather did."

"Still the smug little brat. I kept the wrong twin."

The rug, hell the damn floor, was pulled from underneath him and took what was left of his soul with it. His mother had told him that King hadn't known about his birth. Was it a lie she told herself to feel superior? Or a lie his father told Aaron to keep him in line, using it as a threat or a bargaining chip?

But Aaron was the good son. The one who'd graduated at the top of his class from grade school, and the one who'd doubled the profits at King Enterprises since taking over five years ago, and despite this current stint in rehab, led a clean life. Why did the elder King treat Aaron like shit? Why was Dawson defending his brother?

"Worst deal of your life, huh?" Dawson twirled the pen. "Or maybe I'm just a chip off the old block, as the saying goes." More likely his father was a crappy parent, but Dawson held his tongue for Aaron's sake. Looking out for him, like a real brother would.

No way. More like, the enemy of my enemy is my friend. Yeah, Dawson would stick with that.

## CHAPTER 14

*L*acey paced her office like a lion in a circus cage. She should have expected the former CEO to show up. The Yuen contract was the company's biggest deal. Ever. The injection of cash would allow for the expansion of the more profitable military division. And Dawson had just out-negotiated them all. Fearing his father's displeasure, Aaron never would have risked the sale.

Still, Mr. King's involvement in the day-to-day functions had slipped to an advisory role. So why cut his Monaco trip short? Had Dottie reported back to her former boss about Dawson or rather "Aaron" kissing his executive assistant?

They'd been so careful since Dottie walked in on them, keeping things professional in the office. But sometimes, Lacey laughed a little too loud, or Dawson stood a little too close.

Lacey had been on the lookout for changes in the

employees' treatment of her, but no side-eye glances or knowing smiles had been thrown her way. There was no way anyone, never mind his father, could know about what went on after hours.

Unless Dottie had tuned traitor and had ratted them out, or Edward, who had to suspect that his employer's brother was fooling around with the help. When Dawson did make it back to Aaron's house, it was only for a change of clothes and a shave.

No, she was just being paranoid. Edward would never turn on Aaron or Dawson. This whole ruse was grating on her sanity. And her heart.

She would wish for it to be over, but that meant it would be over with Dawson as well. And that she wasn't ready for.

*Dawson.* How was he holding up under his father's scrutiny?

If only she were a fly on the wall. That wouldn't be good enough though. She needed a way to listen in and talk directly to him.

They needed those earpiece devices the Secret Service used. It was the perfect solution. And while it wouldn't help the cause now, she kept busy by searching online and finding a set that could be delivered tomorrow afternoon.

Pleased she resolved the problem, she opened her email to check on the search for his dog. There was one hit for a German Shepherd named Puss 'n Boots. Boots could be a nickname. But a dog named after a famous fictional cat?

She replied to the email asking for more information about Puss 'n Boots and details about the procedures of adopting and transporting the pup. The cost was no object.

With a little less than three weeks to go, Lacey hoped to give Boots to Dawson as a parting gift. As something to remember her by.

Unless he stayed.

By the way his eyes lit up when Yuen agreed to the six hundred million, Dawson enjoyed the art of the deal as much as Aaron did. Perhaps when the real CEO returned, he'd offer his brother a spot at the company. Would Dawson entertain a position? Not likely.

Lacey had to face the truth. Dawson would return to Alaska with twenty million dollars and her heart. Before she could drown in that truth, Dottie's text pinged on Lacey's phone, giving the all clear.

Risking a broken ankle, she bolted from her office in her sky-high heels. She sputtered to a stop in front of Dottie's desk and said, "Thank you. Anything I should know about?"

"Mr. King wasn't at all happy when he left." Dottie shrugged. "Then again, he never is."

Lacey took a breath. "Please hold all calls."

Peering over her cat-eyed readers with raised brows, Dottie said, "Lock the door."

"We aren't going to—"

"You can't fool me. I've never seen Aaron this happy. It's like he's a different man."

*Oh no!* Damage control Lacey kicked into gear. "Oh, he's just happy the Yuen deal is finalized."

"I wasn't born yesterday. His smile is that of a man in love."

*Love?*

No, Dottie had it wrong. Dawson played the role of CEO well enough, but he couldn't help but let a little of his own personality seep through. So different than stoic Aaron—Dottie mistook it for love, that's all. Just like Lacey did when Dawson held her tight.

After all, who fell in love after a week?

*"You do,"* accused her heart.

*"I'm not in love,"* defended her brain.

Lacey opened the door to the inner sanctum of the kingdom to see Dawson standing by the bank of windows, hands in his pockets and shoulders slumped as if he'd traded places with Atlas.

She locked the door, but not because of Dottie's suggestion. It was time for Dawson to reveal the dark family secret hovering between them.

She walked over and touched his shoulder. "Everything okay?"

"He didn't suspect a thing," he replied, his gaze on the horizon, but a world away.

"That's good. Right? But I meant, are you okay?"

"Me?" He blinked, and then faced her. "Fine. What about you? My father is a cruel man."

"Just another day at the office," she said, smiling though her heart wasn't in it. "How long had it been since you had seen your father?"

"Over twenty years."

Stunned, she said nothing at first. No wonder she,

and the world, had no clue of Dawson's existence. "That would have made you twelve."

"Before that day, I didn't even know I had a twin brother."

"You were separated at birth?"

He nodded. "I was born in Vegas, but my mother is a Canadian citizen, so we'd disappeared there." He took a deep breath. "Anyway, one day, out of the blue, she tells me we're going on a road trip to Disneyland."

Lacey fought the urge to cover her mouth in horror, yet her eyes widened.

"Yeah, you guessed it," Dawson continued. "Instead, of the 'Greatest Place on Earth', after hours of driving, we drove up the long driveway of the King's mansion to meet the man who was my father, who didn't even know I existed."

"How could that be?"

"My mom might have been a showgirl, but she was clever and conniving. She basically sold Aaron and kept me hidden until it suited her. My father couldn't exactly deny I was his, could he? He paid her off to prevent the scandal. And we left."

"That's terrible." Her heart shattered for Dawson. "And what happened between you and Aaron?"

"While our parents argued in the next room, we faced off against each other in a staring contest until..."

"Until what?"

"Let's just say, I wasn't wanted by anyone."

Aaron could be cold-hearted like his father, but how could he be so hateful to his brother? Then again, he'd been only twelve, too. Just a boy frightened that his father's love would be split in two. And a boy who'd just found out he had a mother who hadn't wanted him either. Yes, the blame lay squarely on their twisted parents.

She could never be enough to heal Dawson's hurt or fill the need of the family he so obviously craved. The air between them changed to awkwardness, and she felt his embarrassment as he pulled away. She placed a firm hand on his arm, and he stopped and faced her. His bleak expression tore at her being. Though she couldn't heal his hurt, she could ease his ache if only for a little while.

She put on a cheeky grin. "I want you."

He touched his forehead to hers. "I need you."

By his serious tone, he meant more than the sex, more than her help to continue with the charade.

"I can't wait for tonight," she breathed.

His lips descended onto hers, kissing her as if on a desperate quest to connect with the deepest part of her. And when he arrived there, her heart welled and welcomed him.

"I want to stop time, Lacey. Until all that exists is my hands in your hair, my tongue twined with yours, and I'm buried inside you."

Her breath hitched in response. "I bought us some time," she said, regaining her speech. "I locked the door."

A wicked smile played across his lips. "Couch? Desk? Table?"

The couch would be more comfortable, more hidden. The desk was Aaron's domain. *Stop over-*

*thinking it.* "The table," she said before she could chicken out.

He lifted her up, and she wound her legs around his waist.

"Good, I want to spread you out on it and feast on you," he said as he placed her on the table.

With her skirt already shoved up to her hips, he tugged off her panties. Her pussy pulsed in anticipation of his wet, wicked tongue.

What was she thinking doing the deed during office hours? That was the problem. She wasn't thinking.

At. All.

She was feeling.

All. Over.

Emotions ruled her. Logic, along with her good sense, abandoned her when she needed them most. To shield her heart from Dawson's passionate words, from his coaxing touch, and passionate lovemaking.

This was supposed to be just recreational sex, but it was just a gateway drug to needing more of him. Needing all of him. Body, heart, and soul.

Lacey had planned on a quickie, but Dawson had other ideas, unbuttoning her blouse, nearly tearing the buttons. His lips bruised hers in a crushing kiss, and then ravaged a trail down her neck. He freed her breasts from the cups of her bra.

"Lie back and touch your breasts," he demanded.

Unable to resist, she leaned back. She played with her rock hard nipples, willing him to join her and suck on them.

"Beautiful," he said, his voice husky, filled with need.

*Need.* Her pussy begged for stimulation to ease the painful ache building there. She reached down, but Dawson pushed her hand away. "You said to touch myself."

"Your breasts. This here?" He brushed his thumb down her clit. "Is my job," he said.

"Then get to work." Now it was her turn to command. "Slacker."

He raised his brows. "You're going to pay for that remark." Dawson knelt in front of her. "But not right now." With his hands firmly placed on her thighs, he pulled her closer and then tasted her. "Damn, you're so sweet."

The feelings he evoked as he continued had nothing to do with sweetness and everything to do with heat. With sin. The sunlight pouring onto to the table through the windows warred with the air conditioning, offering no relief to her burning skin as if she was a sacrifice served upon Satan's altar.

What if someone looked up and in from a neighboring building? What if someone was watching them right now? Oh God. Why did that turn her on?

"Dawson." His name slipped from her lips in a gasp. If someone had overheard, all would be lost.

Biting her lip to keep from screaming his name, she drew blood as she came. Freefalling, like she jumped from the roof of this very skyscraper, the shattered fragments of what remained after she landed would leave her forever changed.

# CHAPTER 15

*H*e couldn't bury himself in her heat fast enough. Yet, as he rolled on a condom, he took the time to memorize the way the sunlight illuminated her rosy skin.

With the cups of her pink bra pushed up, exposing her perky breasts, his body rebelled at his poetic musings. Anticipating the feel of her nipples on his tongue, his mouth salivated. Dawson slid his cock along her wet clit, and her body writhed in response.

She offered herself freely, and he accepted, greedily pushing inside her, unleashing a growl of dominance when he filled her completely, like a beast marking his territory. Only this office didn't belong to him. And neither did she.

"Yes!"

"Hook your legs around me, Lacey. It's going to be a bumpy ride."

He needed this. Needed to lose himself in her. To

forget his life before her and be reborn into the man she deserved.

Her wetness surrounded his hard-as-iron cock, allowing him to pound like an animal until her ass bounced off the wood table and her breasts jiggled from the motion. Tonight, he swore he'd make it up to her and take it slow. They were on borrowed time here. Hell, they were on borrowed time period. He'd take every opportunity to feel her heat. To gather each gasp, each kiss, and every breath, to imprint her in his DNA.

Lacey clasped around him, and his balls tightened along with it. The sweet mewing sounds from her lips as she tried to contain her screams would haunt his dreams.

The release rolled over him like barrel waves in a hurricane. He lost himself within her, but at the same time, found a home he'd been yearning for.

Without her, he would once again be adrift in an ocean of loneliness.

Anyone who believed it was better to have loved and lost than to have never loved at all was a fool. And he was the biggest fool of them all. But at least he now knew he was human and capable of loving another.

Once their breathing evened, he helped her off the table.

Righting her clothes, she smiled shyly, glancing at him from underneath her eyelashes. "That was indeed bumpy."

He zipped up his pants. *Fuck*. Had he gone too far? He hadn't meant to be a brute, but he couldn't exactly say he was sorry. "I love the way you come."

"I paying for it now." Lacey hobbled to the door and unlocked it.

On her way back, Dawson grinned, smacking her ass as she walked by him. "No pain, no gain."

"Ow! As if my ass doesn't hurt enough."

"I'll baby it tonight."

"You should go home in case your father shows up."

Crap, had he ruined what was building between them by being a caveman? He swore he'd be gentle next time, no matter how much she drove him to the brink of madness. "So, stay over."

"I better not."

"You wouldn't be saying that if I hadn't just rocked your world," he said as a test to gauge how much he'd fucked up.

"The world?" She shook her head. "Maybe the state of California," she added with a saucy smile.

"Like the 'Big One'?"

"Yes, ten points on the Richter Scale." She giggled. "Now, play time is over. Back to work." She picked up the folders that had been swept to the carpet in the heat of the moment. "And if you're lucky, we'll have another tryst before we leave." She placed the folders on the table. "But this time on the couch."

* * *

LATER THAT NIGHT, after an overtime romp up against the windows of the office, Dawson entered Aaron's deserted house. Though it was filled with expensive things, it held no warmth. No Lacey.

Dwelling on how lonely Alaska would be without her would do him no good, but left alone, his thoughts dogged him. What once was his sanctuary would now be his prison. His soul, no longer desolate like the frozen tundra, craved Lacey's warm touch. His heart, no longer encased in ice, burned for her love. She had changed everything.

But was that enough to keep him in L.A.? Maybe. Was it enough to stand by and watch her work for his brother? No way.

Yet he respected her work ethic and accomplishments at King Enterprises too much to ask her to give up her career.

Or was he just afraid she'd say no?

He heard a noise from the kitchen. Grateful to have his train of thought derailed, he made his way through the house to see the butler by the stove.

"Hello, Edward."

"Hello, Dawson. Everything okay with you and Lacey?"

That was a loaded question. He avoided the answer at all costs. "Father showed up. Still the same prick that I remember."

The butler nodded as he carefully poured warm milk into a mug. "I would have left his employ a long time ago, but I stayed for Aaron's sake."

"Why? He had everything."

"Everything but love. Aaron might as well have been an orphan."

"I hope you don't expect me to feel sorry for him."

"No, but I expect you to understand why he is the way he is. Aaron changed after you met."

"What does it matter? It's not like we're going to be best bros once this is over."

"That's too bad."

Dawson thought Edward was going to argue the point.

"And what about you and Lacey?"

*Fuck me.* Dawson would much rather talk about his non-relationship with Aaron than the developing one with Lacey. Each day, they grew closer as they revealed bits and pieces of themselves. Some fit together while others would never match unless something was cut away.

Even if Lacey felt the same, who was she falling in love with? Dawson played his role with flawless accuracy, allowing him to hide his real self behind the suit, the hair, and the clean-shaven face. Only in bed, stripped of more than his clothes, he bared his soul.

While he knew she wasn't a gold digger like his father accused, no woman wanted a man who couldn't provide the basics. With twenty million dollars he could do that and more, but he considered the money tainted. There was no pride in living off his brother's money, which was why he was using it for good.

He'd only agreed to this charade so he could help the veterans in his community, find his dog, and buy a truck. Damn, he sounded like a country song in the making.

How could he expect Lacey, a Harvard grad and an

executive assistant of a Fortune 500 company, to follow a high school graduate bar owner to Alaska? In addition to those faults, his PTSD could rear its ugly head at any time.

But there was one thing he could give her more of than any other man breathing—orgasms.

Edward raised his brow. "Dawson?"

"I'm in love with her."

To his surprise, Edward nodded his approval.

"So what are you going to do about it?"

Could Dawson swallow his pride? For Lacey, yes, he would. Could he risk his heart? "I don't know."

"As your generation says 'put on a ring on it.'"

He tried to imagine the life Edward dangled in front of him. Dawson had always thought he'd be alone. It was how he was made. It didn't matter what he wanted, it was what Lacey needed—deserved —that did.

Orgasms only qualified him for a position as a gigolo, not a husband.

# CHAPTER 16

*H*aving rushed to the office in hopes of getting in a quickie before the employees arrived, Lacey's pussy ached in disappointment to find that Dawson hadn't been of the same mind.

She craved the buzz in her blood and the rapid beat of her heart whenever she was in his presence. She'd been caught off guard by just how much she missed him. Her plan to use his father as an excuse to put some distance between them had failed miserably. Whether it was ten miles or a thousand, the result was the same.

Without his warm body sprawled out beside her, she'd been unable to sleep. She knew she better get used to it. In a couple of weeks, her bed would be empty and cold. Her life, which she once thought was so full, would be, too. At least she would have the title she coveted. But being vice president wouldn't keep her warm at night. Or make her smile like a lovesick fool. Or give her Rock 'Em Sock 'Em orgasms.

"Hey there."

Lacey jumped in her seat, even though she'd been expecting him. Dawson stood at the doorway, holding a cup of coffee, looking like hell, but a sexy hell, one she would follow him into. The only thing that would make him sexier was if the coffee was for her. "Couldn't sleep either?"

"Not a wink." He strode across the office, placed the mug on the table as he bent over to kiss her. Stealing her breath, and along with it, her heart. There was no mistaking that he'd missed her as much as she'd missed him. She inhaled the taste of coffee and desire.

"Tonight, you're coming home with me," he ordered.

She nodded, but before she could kiss him back, she heard Dottie clearing her throat outside by the secretary's desk.

"Damn it," said Dawson.

"Well, you're the one who was late," she said. "Where's my coffee?"

"No coffee for you. Punishment for abandoning me last night." Dawson's brow furrowed.

Was he thinking about how his father had deserted him? Did he really think that's what she was doing? He was the one who was leaving. "I believe withholding coffee is against the Geneva Convention."

"Perhaps you would prefer a spanking?" A hopeful gleam sparked in his eyes, setting off a firestorm of want inside her.

"Perhaps I would," she said with a half-smile.

"Duly noted."

* * *

LATER IN THE DAY, the secretary knocked and walked in with a package. "This came for you, Miss Brooks."

"Thank you, Dottie." Lacey stood and met her halfway.

"Mr. King, would you like more tea?"

"No, thanks. Why don't you take the rest of the day off?"

Dottie raised a brow before turning to the door, but then stopped. "Aaron?"

Now it was Lacey's turn to raise a brow. The secretary hardly ever referred to the boss as anything other than Mr. King.

"I've been thinking of retiring."

Oh boy. If Lacey had any hopes of leaving the company to follow Dawson—not that she had decided to—not that he asked—Dottie couldn't leave. Aaron would have a fit. Before Dawson could be Mr. Nice Guy and accept, she stepped forward and said, "Please consider staying on for another year."

"But you two seem so settled. I don't think I'm needed anymore."

Dawson leaned forward in the chair. "Dottie, you no doubt earned your retirement ten times over, but you are needed, more than you know. And appreciated."

Dottie's face brightened, and her shoulders straightened. "Why, thank you, Aaron." She left closing the door behind her.

Lacey's own shoulders slumped with relief. "We dodged a bullet."

"No doubt. My brother's transition from rehab to work will be smoother with Dottie here."

Lacey felt like a traitor for even considering leaving King Enterprises. But wouldn't she be betraying her heart by not following it? *Stop obsessing. It's not like Dawson has declared his undying love for you.*

"What's that?" Dawson nodded to the package.

"Oh. Actually, it's for you. Us. A present."

Dawson's eyes lit up like a kid at Christmas. He shook the FedEx box. "Shouldn't it be wrapped?"

Perhaps she shouldn't have called it a present. "Just open it."

Dawson dumped the contents out on the desk. "Huh?"

"It's a Bluetooth spy ear thingy set." She rested a hip on the desk. "You know, in case your father shows up again and I get kicked out. We'll be able to communicate."

Dawson leaned back in the chair, looking up at her like that kid on Christmas who hadn't gotten his wish. "You suck at presents. Memo for next time: lingerie —red."

"I don't think it comes in your size," she said with a smirk.

"Thank God."

"Speedo?"

"A crime against man." He placed a hand firmly on her thigh, drifting up until his thumb played along the hem of her skirt. "Besides, I think you know what I mean."

She leaned in, flipping the top button of her blouse to reveal the lace of her purple bra. "I do."

"It's not red."

She straightened. "Spoiled brat."

Dawson chuckled deep in his throat. "I've never been accused of that before."

She winced, feeling rotten to the core. He'd grown up with so little. Lifting one of the buds, she placed it in her ear. "What if I promise to whisper sweet nothings in your ear?"

"Sweet nothings?" Dawson picked up the other one. "Make it dirty talk, and we have a deal."

"Wow, you are born to be a negotiator like your bro..." Her eyes widened. "I'm sorry. That was a really stupid thing to say. So was teasing that you're spoiled."

Dawson shrugged. "I can take it." He fiddled with the small electronic pack that attached to a belt clip. "This is a better quality than I used in the military."

"That's terrible."

He shrugged again. "I'm used to doing a lot with a little. So should we do a test run?"

"Later." She glanced over at his computer. A real estate website was up. "What are you doing?"

"I'm looking into this building."

Lacey stood and placed a hand on his shoulder as she scanned the listing for a large, commercial building. "Are you expanding the bar?"

"No. I'm starting a veterans shelter."

Most men would be planning to purchase high-end

cars, mansions, and giant televisions. She'd teased him about being spoiled and being like his brother while he was the most selfless man she'd ever known.

And he was returning to Alaska. A sickening pit grew in her stomach.

Dawson looked over his shoulder. "I could use some help setting things up."

Was this his way of asking her to go with him? Hopeful excitement sprinkled like fairy dust around her.

"You know with contracts and setting up a charity."

That fairy dust morph to deaden ash in a flash. God, she was becoming Bi-Polar, her moods swinging in hurricane force winds. She didn't have to move to Alaska to volunteer her time. How could she be so ready to ditch all that she'd worked for? To give it up like her mother had? Only love did that. And that made love dangerous.

"You know, if Aaron doesn't mind."

"What I do in my personal time is my own business." She tilted her head and shook her finger at Dawson. "Wait a minute." Was he using psychology to get her to do what he wanted? "I know what you're doing." She put her hands on her hips. "Damn, you *are* just like your brother."

"That cuts me deep. But the perks of working for me outweigh the fringe benefits here."

"Ah! I have stellar healthcare."

"So do I. It's called 'An orgasm a day keeps the doctor away.'"

She held in a laugh. "Just one?" she pouted.

"Now who's spoiled?"

* * *

ANOTHER WEEK, another charity benefit. When had she become so jaded? This one was for the L.A. homeless, reminding Lacey of Dawson's generosity and the lunacy of such dinners. People should just give. Not because its good publicity or good business, but because it was the right thing to do.

She was quite the hypocrite. The cost of her outfit alone could feed a family of four for a month.

Underneath the sparkling black gown, she wore red lingerie as a surprise for Dawson. With the earpieces in use, she could hear him speaking with the head of Ian Security, who was vying for a government contract, as she made her away to the ladies room. She had just dried her hands when Dawson's husky bedroom voice spoke in her ear.

"Are you alone?"

And that was all it took to get her to slick with wet heat. "Yes."

"I've been dying to touch you all night. You'll have to do it for me. Now."

"Now? What if someone walks in?"

"That's part of the fun."

She returned to the farthest stall and locked it. "Ready."

"Are you?"

She leaned against the tiled sidewall. "Yes."

"Good. If it were me, I'd tear the sexy slit of your dress all the way to your hip."

"Not happening," she giggled.

"That's okay. I'll do it later. For now, push the slit to the side and then ride your hand up your thigh to the band of your panties."

Was she really going to do this? Apparently she was, and followed his instructions.

"Tease your fingers along the band."

Her pussy tingled in anticipation.

"What color?"

She knew exactly what he was asking. "Same as my bra. Red."

"Holy hell."

"What now?"

"Slip two fingers in and touch yourself."

She could probably come just from his whispered directions. She bit her lip but a sound escaped. "Mmmm."

"Play with your clit."

"Mmmm...mmmm."

"Is it wet and plump?"

"Yes," she breathed.

"Good. Slide those two fingers in your beautiful pussy."

"Dawson..." Her breath hitched.

"Do it. Pretend it's me. My cock. Pumping inside you."

She couldn't speak. She couldn't think. He ruled her body like a puppet master. Instead of pulling her strings, he sang to them. The tune hummed, then vibrated through her, growing louder with each lyric.

"Swirl your thumb over your clit."

"Oh, oh, God." Only it wasn't God whispering into her ear. It was Satan.

"Lacey, I'm so hard for you right now."

She was dying to come but held back, afraid once she did, she wouldn't be able to stop. Wouldn't be able to stop moaning. "Please," she prayed.

"Come on, babe. Let. Go."

Lightening torched through her body, and she came in glorious waves of release.

After a moment, a minute, an hour, or an eternity, she was able to utter, "Wow."

"Oh, man, that was so hot."

His laugh, low and dangerous, seeped into the neurons of her mind, creating connections to Dawson's. Or so it seemed.

She half expected to open her eyes and see him before her. When she did, she blinked, forgetting where she was.

She righted her clothes then stepped out to wash her hands. She glanced down the row of stalls, hoping no one had come in while she was lost in the haze of the heat Dawson had spurred her to. As she soaped up her hands, she gazed in the mirror. With her skin glowing, her cheeks flushed, and her eyes wide, but misty, there was no need to re-apply makeup. "Where are you?"

"Guarding the door, dying a slow torturous death."

She stopped fussing with her appearance, walked to

the exit, and flung open the door. Dawson's broad back greeted her.

"Why didn't you tell me you were out here?"

He turned, sporting a devastating grin as he eyed her toe-to-head. "Because it turned me on that you were doing yourself thinking at any moment someone could walk in."

"You should have joined me." She slid a finger along the back of his ear where the device was in. "So not such a bad present after all, huh?"

"Best gift ever," he said before dragging her into a deserted conference room.

Now if she could only find his dog.

# CHAPTER 17

*H*e was a chicken shit.

For days, he'd failed to speak the words lingering on the tip of his tongue. He almost said them out loud, earlier, when she was out of the office, to let the phrase fly through the airwaves into her earpiece. *I love you.*

Now, he studied Lacey at the table as she finalized the offer on the Alaskan building while he sat useless behind the desk. Yep, he was a shit to add his crap to her already mind-numbing workload at King Enterprises.

It could've waited until he was free of this place, but he didn't want to be free of Lacey. Ever. He could've hired lawyers and experts to navigate a charity startup. Asking for her help had been the coward's way of keeping her connected to him. Perhaps a clean break would have been better.

At least he'd have the veterans' shelter to pour what

was left of his heart into.

His father roared into the office, slamming the door. Today, he was dressed less formally in striped navy pants and a white polo shirt. Like he'd just stepped off a golf course.

"So you didn't think I would find out."

Dawson dragged in a fortifying breath. "Find out what?"

"Don't patronize me. Your brother is in rehab."

From the corner of his eye, he noticed Lacey had stood, her back and shoulders rigid, her eyes wide.

Dawson shrugged, feeling his way through this unexpected development. "He didn't want you to know."

While he would never expect—or welcome—his father's embrace, neither did he imagine King would ignore that the brothers had traded places, and his other son, who he hadn't seen in twenty years, stood right in front of him.

As realization dawned, he fought to keep his expression neutral. Aaron had used Dawson's name to check-in. His father thought Dawson was the one in rehab. The hit of his brother's betrayal was nothing compared to Lacey's.

*But she didn't know you.*

"I'm his father," King bellowed.

"Biologically speaking."

"I'm going to buy the mortgage on his bar and shut him down."

"I already paid it off." It was the first thing he'd done with his advance.

"Then you shut him down."

"No. It's his livelihood. Besides, he's not alcoholic."

"It doesn't matter. His drug supplier is part of that seedy element his bar attracts."

Dawson's hands fisted. Staying silent was the only way to keep the rising anger in check. If his father knew who Aaron's supplier was, he wouldn't be so smug. The rich were such hypocrites.

Why was Dawson protecting Aaron? He obviously wouldn't do the same for him. If his father followed through, he would lose the bar. And if he were honest, the thought that the prick thought Dawson was an addict enraged him.

He could almost understand why his brother had done what he had. If King could take Dawson's bar, what would he do to Aaron? Take the company back? Well, fuck Aaron. But if Aaron was out as CEO, then was Lacey out of a job? He'd protect his brother for her, even if she was part of the deception.

"Did you hear me?"

Dawson looked up.

"I'm reporting him to Alaska's liquor board and getting his license pulled."

His blood boiled. Through clenched teeth he responded, "You won't. He'll hate you."

"He already hates me, as do you."

"You kept me away from my brother. My twin!" He was speaking as Dawson now.

"What is she doing here?"

"I work here."

Dawson smiled, proud that she'd finally stood up

for herself.

"Sir, you will let me handle this. He's getting help. If you start poking your nose where it doesn't belong, the word will get out about our family shame—and if you touch his bar or my company, I'll make sure it does."

"You wouldn't dare!"

Dawson shrugged. "If not me, then I'm sure your other son would, especially if you interfere with his life."

His father shook a finger. "This isn't over."

Without waiting for a response, he strode out of the office, leaving the door open. Dawson walked over and closed it after telling Dottie to hold all calls.

"What the fuck, Lacey?" He walked over to where she stood.

"What?"

"My father thinks I'm the one in rehab."

"I thought you knew." She looked down, running a hand along the stack of files in front of her. "What does it matter?"

Speechless, he stared at her. The silence stretched out between them like the vast void of space.

"It's just a name," she explained, looking him in the eye.

*Just a name?* He turned away from her and paced the office. The silence exploded like the big bang. "That's all I have, Lacey. Aaron stole everything. My father. My home. My life." Deep down, he knew Aaron wasn't the cause, but he was the benefactor.

"My name was all I had," he continued on his rampage. "And I might not be the pillar of society, but I fought for my country. And now I'm being dragged through the mud."

"I'm sorry. Truly, I am, and I wish things had been handled differently, but you signed a contract."

"Stupid high school graduate that I am."

"Dawson, that's not the way I see you."

He stopped and looked at her. "It's the way you saw me when you walked into my bar."

"I—"

"Be honest."

"Only because I didn't know the reasons why you weren't part of Aaron's life, I thought…I thought you might be a criminal," she admitted.

Her words cut deep into his soul. *Well I wanted honesty, didn't I?* "Yet, you work for someone as unethical as my brother?"

"Aaron isn't the monster you think he is."

"Wow. At least I know where I stand."

"No. Dawson, I—"

"I'm taking the rest of day off." He grabbed the keys to the Porsche off the desk.

"I'll come with you. We can talk about this," she pleaded.

He turned so he couldn't see the tears forming in her eyes. "No. This is where you belong. King Enterprises is lucky to have such a loyal employee, and Aaron is lucky to have a loyal friend."

"It's not like that."

"Yes, it is," he said, his tone flat, resigned to the fact they could never work. If he was being honest with himself it was the real cause of his anger.

# CHAPTER 18

*L*acey could only watch as Dawson stormed out of the office much the way his father had come in. She tried to work up enough righteous indignation to evaporate the water swimming in her eyes. Dawson witnessed the world in black and white while she saw shades of gray. It was so much more than the miles that would keep them apart.

Dottie hustled into the room. "What was that all about?"

The gathering tears spilled over. She never cried at work. Never. "I've made a mess of things."

Dottie hugged her and gave her a little shake. "Don't give up on him. You two were meant for one another."

"You don't understand," said Lacey. Dottie thought Dawson was Aaron. How simple everything would be if he were. While her business acumen and negotiation skills were an asset to Aaron, to Dawson they were her fatal flaw. This was who she was. But it's not want she wanted to be. Not any longer.

Dottie patted her hand. "I understand love."

"I don't." To Lacey, love made no sense at all. Why did it turn a sane, smart woman into crazy stupid female? Why did it turn your world upside down? Make you want. Make you need. "Shouldn't love be the simplest of emotions?"

"I find it's usually people who make it harder than it has to be," the secretary advised sagely. "Why don't you take the rest of the day off?"

Though she craved to go home and crawl into bed, it wouldn't look good to the employees. Neither would the tear tracks left on her face. "Thanks, Dottie, but no, I'm going to freshen up and then head to my office."

Looking and feeling human again, she plopped into her desk chair and opened up her email. She groaned at the size of her inbox, scrolling down to see if anything seemed urgent. Hope rose as she clicked on one from OMSD, an organization who matched military service dogs to adopted families. After scanning the email, she twirled in her chair in joy.

* * *

FROM HOME, Lacey worked out the final details of adopting Boots. Maybe this would show Dawson how much she cared. Excitement buzzed through her with the last of the paperwork approved. Boots was theirs—no, Dawson's. Funny how she'd easily slipped into being a couple, as if they were on the road to wedded bliss.

But at least he couldn't be mad at her now. Once he was reunited with his dog, he'd overlook her wheelings and dealings for King Enterprises. After all, those connections cut through the mounds of red tape that Dawson would have encountered if he'd even found the dog.

The doorbell rang. She ran to open it. Dawson stood looking disheveled—broken. She'd done that. She should've had his back. Instead, she'd defended herself when all he wanted was her understanding.

She jumped into his arms, and he caught her, holding her to him like he was never going to let her go.

"I'm sorry that I left like that," he murmured into her hair. "Sorry I lashed out at you."

"I understand, I do. I sacrificed the best parts of myself on the altar of getting ahead."

"No, you're wonderful." He pulled away slightly as her toes touched the ground, but still held her as he gazed into her eyes. "This isn't your fault. I'm a brute and a lout for taking my past out on you."

"Dawson, you're a good man."

"Right now, I don't feel much like one."

"We had an argument."

Her phone pinged. She jumped back in the house to see the text, hoping it was from Simms. "The jet is ready. Let's go."

"Wait. What? Where are we going?"

"You'll see." She grabbed her purse from the kitchen counter. She stepped back outside and locked the door.

"Are you taking me home?"

"Alaska?" Lacey's heart dropped as her brows furrowed. "No, is that where you want to go?" She could hear the disappointment in her voice.

Dawson's eyes widened. "No, no. I'll see this through."

With her heart back in its proper place, she said, "Good, but you'll have to wait and see. I want it to be a surprise."

\* \* \*

WHEN THE SEATBELT light over the pilot's cabin door went off, Dawson leaned forward. "Is Aaron coming home early?"

"Gosh, you're impatient. Don't you like surprises?"

"In my former line of work, surprises were never good."

"Oh." Then Lacey raised a suspicious brow. "Hey, are you trying to make me feel guilty?"

"Is it working?"

"Yes." Lacey paused for dramatic effect. "I found Boots."

A brief look of shock crossed his face, followed by an ear-to-ear smile. "How? And we're going to get him now?"

"I had trouble tracking him down since I didn't have his full name, but yes. There's a discharge center in St. Louis."

"Thank you, Lacey." He shook his head, his eyes full of amazement.

"It's nothing." She squeezed his hand. "Something to remember me by."

"I have every moment with you engraved in my memory. Each touch, each kiss, each sigh, each time..." His voice broke, and he kissed her hand. "I've been pretending to be something I'm not, but know this Lacey, my feelings for you are real." Then he placed her hand on his heart. "This is real."

She wanted to break open her heart and lay it bare, but with the way his eyes had lit when he'd asked about Alaska, about Aaron coming home early, she kept it sewn shut.

Lacey stood, still holding his hand. "Let's make another memory," she said, nodding to the back room of the jet where a queen-sized bed awaited. "Wanna make me a member of the mile-high club?"

He held a hand over his heart. "It would be my sacred honor."

With reverence and patience, he worshipped her body until his essence had seeped into her very being, settled there, and became a part of her.

# CHAPTER 19

Standing at the kennel's adoption desk, Dawson rubbed his palms together. Why was he as nervous as that young boy who'd faced his first day of combat? This was a good day. One Lacey had arranged, and like the angel she was, she placed a reassuring hand on his shoulder.

"They're bringing him out now," said the receptionist.

But Boots hung by the door, skittish and unsure. So unlike the happy but disciplined dog he'd served with. Dawson's guilty heart broke. He didn't deserve Lacey, but Boots belonged with him. But right now the dog wouldn't come to him.

Perhaps it was the suit? Without the uniform or beard, Dawson must appear to be yet another stranger in the dog's path to a forever home.

"Come on, Boots. It's okay, it's me, Trudeau."

Whether the dog recognized his voice, the name, or both, he sprung forward like a puppy chasing after a thrown bone.

Dawson scuffed his neck as the dog whined, and then rolled over for his all-time favorite—the belly rub. Dawson spoke nonsensical words to his best buddy.

He thought his face might break from smiling. Happy as he was to see Boots, the memories—always in back of his mind—rushed front and center. The battles, the skirmishes, the bullets, the bombs, and the unforgiving heat. But that was over—in the past—for the both of them. Boots was going to love Alaska.

"You're coming home with me."

Back on all fours, Boots licked Dawson's face in agreement.

He introduced Lacey, and she held out her hand to take his paw.

"Hi, Boots."

The dog had his own way of greeting a female. Ignoring her hand, Boots eagerly sniffed Lacey's crotch.

"Whoa, boy."

"Sorry. If you haven't guessed, that's how he got his name."

"Typical man." Lacey's tone was one of exasperation, but her tears were undeniably ones of joy.

Damn, if he wasn't tearing up himself.

* * *

WITH ONE WEEK LEFT, Dawson stood by the window, gazing out at the skyline, pondering his future. Though he would be a rich man when this was over, without Lacey, he might as well be a beggar in the streets.

Boots barked and pranced around the office. Used to wide-open spaces, the dog was just like his owner.

"You should have left him with Edward." Lacey continued to review the contracts at the conference table. "We're lucky the staff bought your ridiculous 'He's the new King Enterprises mascot' story."

Dawson knew she was right, but he hadn't been able to refuse those pleading, sad eyes. He imagined himself with the same expression when it was time to leave Lacey.

And like a dog seeking attention, he snatched the papers from her hand. "Let's go for a walk in the park."

Boots' ears perked.

"You go," said Lacey, trying to grab the contract back.

Boots whined, crawling underneath the table to sniff between her legs.

"Oh!"

Yep, he and his dog were of the same mind.

"Stop that! Okay, okay. I'll go!"

Once they reached the lobby, the beast bounded ahead. At first Dawson thought the boy was anxious to leave, but something had gained the dog's attention.

Fear gripped Dawson's heart when Boots started sniffing the floor.

The dog's haunches stiffened. As Dawson drew

closer, he noticed a black backpack resting against a marble column. *Fuck me.*

Boots sat and flicked his tail just like he'd been trained to do.

"Are you sure, boy?" he asked, even though he already knew. The pup had saved his unit's lives time and time again. Boots crooked his head to look at him and then stared straight ahead. "We have to evacuate the building."

"What? Why?" Lacey asked.

Dawson's first instinct was to drag Lacey to safety, but instead, he grabbed her by the elbow and pulled her to the security guard's station. "Hector, sound the fire alarm."

Without a pause, the man who was ex-military, calmly said, "Right away, Mr. King."

"Where's the fire?" asked Lacey, looking around the lobby.

Dawson held up one hand, and with the other, he grabbed the phone on the guard's desk and called 9-1-1.

The operator answered. "What's your emergency?"

Dawson relayed the address and who he was, using Aaron's name. "There's an unattended backpack in the lobby. A former service dog in Afghanistan has flagged it as a threat—a bomb."

With wide, fearful eyes, Lacey mouthed the word 'bomb'?

"Yes, we are evacuating." He nodded as he hung up with 9-1-1.

The alarm blared. Boots nipped at his pants legs.

"Lacey, promise me you'll leave right now," he shouted over the piercing noise.

"What? Why? Aren't you coming?" Her voice pitched with desperation.

"I have to make sure our floor is clear."

"That's not your job."

"Yes, it is." Even as the fake CEO, his responsibility for the employees was real. "Now, promise me."

"Promise me you'll be okay," said Lacey.

"This isn't a negotiation." He turned her toward the exit and smacked her on her ass. "Now go."

The concern etched on her face when she looked back made him want to follow. Before he did exactly that, he jabbed a finger at the door. "Go."

He had never left a man behind, and he wasn't about to start now.

Despite this, he waited until Lacey exited the building. When she was out of sight, he spotted Hector directing the public to the side exits away from the backpack by the main entrance. "Make sure Miss Brooks doesn't sneak her way back in here."

"Yes, sir."

"Come on, Boots. We just came out of retirement."

The elevators were currently working, but he knew that wouldn't last. He decided to chance it. With Boots by his side, they wormed their way into the car just as it emptied of the frantic people pushing out.

The doors slid closed. He hit the fifty-fifth floor button. The familiar rush of adrenaline pumped through his veins, and so did the creeping anxiety. The small space enclosed around him, and panic replaced the adrenaline. Then he felt a snout rubbing against his legs, jolting him out of the doom descending upon him. Boots wasn't a therapy dog, but he recognized his owner's distress. Dawson dropped to one knee and hugged the hero of the day, heaping praise upon the pup.

"Thanks, Boots."

The dog answered by licking his face. The elevator jolted to a stop. Fearing it would proceed to the ground floor, he reached over and hit the emergency stop button. He pried the doors open. Relieved to find there was just enough room squeeze through, he lifted Boots to the opening first and pulled himself up and out. Five floors short of his destination, they sprinted up the stairs, pushing past the people rushing down.

Flinging the door open, he wasn't at all surprised to see some of Aaron's employees still working as if the fire alarm had never sounded. Dawson clapped his hands and shouted over the noise.

"Come on, people. This isn't a drill. Out!"

The remaining staff scattered to the exit. He then went cubicle to cubicle, sweeping the area like he was on a mission back in Afghanistan. He was about to leave when he heard typing coming from the hall leading to his office. It had to be Aaron's secretary.

"Uh, Dottie, didn't you get the memo?"

"Mr. King? You should be outside."

"So should you." Without another word, he rolled Dottie's chair, with her still sitting in it, down the hallway toward the stairwell.

"The elevators are out," she sniffed.

"We're taking the stairs."

"I'll never make it."

"Yes, *we* will," he promised.

"But—"

"Hold on." He hefted Dottie over his shoulder into a fireman's carry. "This may get bumpy," he said and began the long descent.

"No! I'm an old woman. Save yourself."

"For an old woman, you sure do have a nice ass," he noted as a way to get her mind off their current circumstances.

"Now you get a sense of humor?"

At the thirtieth floor, he stopped, his legs on fire and his lungs laboring for air. "You okay, Dottie?"

"I hope the health insurance covers hip replacements. I'm going to need one or two."

"Sorry."

"And not that I'm ungrateful, but I'm retiring at the end of the day."

"Me, too." He took a deep breath. Shook out his legs. "Ready?"

Without waiting for an answer, he continued down. By the twentieth floor, the burn in his legs cooled to lead. Each weighted step felt like walking on the ocean floor. Even Boots panted, his tongue lolling to the side.

"It's okay, boy," Dawson encouraged, though it was difficult to speak. What if he hadn't agreed to switch places with Aaron? What if his kind-hearted Lacey hadn't pursued and found his dog? What if he hadn't taken Boots to work today? So many ifs. It couldn't be a coincidence. Fate had led him here. To this exact moment. And not to save the occupants of this building, but to save him from a life without love.

Of that, he was now sure.

The thought of Lacey waiting at bottom strengthened his resolve to soldier on.

# CHAPTER 20

Knowing she'd only get in the way, Lacey raced out of the building, even though she had never actually promised to do so. She paced the sidewalk as the alarms continued to blare. The police arrived within minutes, setting up barricades across the street, ordering her, and the crowd that had gathered, behind them.

"If you're smart, you'll go home," shouted a cop. "We have to be here, you don't."

Lacey tried talking her way past the bright yellow barriers, throwing her position at King Enterprises around like it should grant her special access, but the cops didn't see it that way.

"You don't understand. Aar..." She said to the nearest two officers, but stopped herself. There was no way in hell she'd let Aaron take credit for Dawson's bravery.

"A veteran, who served in Afghanistan, and his

service dog found the backpack. They went back in to help evacuate the building."

A seasoned and weathered cop said, "Jesus H. Christ. To survive that hell hole only to come home to this?"

His younger partner glared at him, then gazed at her. "Look, lady, I wouldn't worry. I'm sure your boyfriend knows what he's doing."

Boyfriend? *Was I that transparent?* And Dawson was more than that insipid title. He was her everything. And she'd never told him how she felt.

The bomb squad raced into the main entrance as the last of the employees streamed out of the side exits. Where was he? Then she remembered the earpiece she wore. She turned it on. "Dawson!"

"Lacey, are you okay?" he asked, his breathing labored.

"Yes, I'm outside. Where are you?"

"I'm helping Dottie down the stairs."

That sweet, brave man! Dottie had to be pushing seventy. It would take them forever to make it down fifty-five flights. What if the unthinkable happened?

"Dawson, I love you." There. It was out in the universe.

Only the universe answered back with a crackle of static.

"Dawson?" Silence. "I can't reach him," she said to the cop, tapping her earpiece.

"They probably cut the radio signal to prevent a remote denotation."

Denotation? Short panicky breaths produced tears.

Lacey bit on her lip to prevent an anguished cry from escaping, knowing it would turn into an all-out breakdown. Even with the sea of people crowding her, she'd never felt more alone.

Practicing what she preached to Aaron, she closed her eyes in not only meditation but prayer. Though the world around her was in utter chaos, she willed herself still. Minutes ticked by, but they felt like a lifetime. She pleaded with the universe, with God, for everyone's safety.

A dog barked in answer to her prayer.

As she opened her eyes, a hopeful sight greeted her. Boots sprinted toward her. She crouched down to scruff his neck. "Good dog."

Her gaze lifted, desperately searching for a glimpse of his owner. Like a dream, Dawson appeared on the main steps with Dottie slung across one shoulder. Lacey stood, her heart clenched. Strong in form and in character, Dawson was a hero in the truest sense of the word. Tears pricked her eyes again, but this time, they were ones of relief.

"That's him," Lacey said to the cops. "Let me through."

"Sorry, lady."

So achingly close, yet so painfully far. Didn't they understand she needed to physically touch him to make sure he was okay? That he was real?

Dawson gently placed Dottie down by an ambulance and patted her hand. Then he looked into the crowd.

Waving like a woman stranded on a deserted island

flagging down a ship in the distance, she half yelled, half cried, "Dawson!"

Spotting her, he smiled and waved back. He jogged over, gesturing to the crowd to move back. He jumped over the barrier, and the spectators scrambled to make room.

His strong hands fell to her shoulders. "I love you, too," he said, out of breath. He dragged in a long gulp of air, then continued, "Move to Alaska with me. Marry me?"

Her inner voice shut the hell up for once. All the doubts and misgivings faded. She didn't care if she was that woman who gave it all up for a man. Because that man was Dawson.

Her career, and the prestige and money that went along with it, meant nothing without him. What she was receiving in return made all those things seem petty and small. This man—his love was vital and huge. Tears of relief turned to tears of happiness.

"Yes!"

The crowd cheered.

"Only in LA," said the veteran cop.

Dawson eyes went wide, as if he'd expected her to say no.

"What about your promotion? Your job?"

"I'll telecommute until Aaron finds a replacement."

"There's one problem, Lacey. There's no replacing you."

"So true," she said with a cheeky smile. "But he'll survive." Stroking Dawson's cheek, she turned serious. "While I can't breathe without you."

"You sure that's not the LA smog?"

"Hey, are you trying to wiggle your way out of your marriage proposal?"

"No way. I'm ready to negotiate the terms of my surrender."

"This is not negotiation," she said, happily throwing his earlier words back at him. "It's an ironclad, lifetime contract with no escape clause."

"Where do I sign?"

Lacey pointed to her lips. "Right here."

His lips upon hers sealed more than the deal. Two hearts—two souls now sealed together in one kiss.

# EPILOGUE

Dawson gazed out at the LA concrete jungle. In two days, he'd be back in the forests of Alaska, breathing in clean air and sweet freedom. That freedom would have meant nothing without Lacey by his side. In fact, it wouldn't have been freedom at all.

The bush would be a culture shock for the savvy businesswoman. For her to trade in high-heels for hiking boots, office fashion for flannel, and multi-million dollar deals for applying for grants and fundraising, meant the world to him. He hoped he would be worthy of her sacrifice.

The office phone rang.

Hoping it was his contact at Homeland Security, who had taken possession of defused device, he strode to the desk. Though he suspected the bomb had been planted because of King Enterprises' military division, no one had claimed responsibility for the bomb. No group would admit to such a failure. And that failure was all thanks to Boots, who was underneath the desk, gnawing on a bone.

"Aaron King," Dawson answered.

"You wish," said his brother.

"Not on my worst day," Dawson replied. There was nothing left to wish for anyway. He had it all.

"Well, hell, sometimes I don't want to be me either."

"I hope you don't expect me to feel sorry for you."

"I'd kill you if you did."

Panic punched Dawson's gut. What if Aaron needed to extend his stay? "You're coming home tomorrow. Right?"

"Fuck yeah, but I need you to jet down here tomorrow. Lacey, too."

"What for?"

"I have to do the Amends bullshit."

"Bullshit, huh?" Dead silence followed, and he thought Aaron had hung up. "Bro?"

"Please."

Hearing the strangled plea, Dawson knew it wasn't bullshit. "Of course, we'll be there."

"Good," said Aaron, once again composed. "I'll see you tomorrow then. Around eleven."

"Wait, aren't you going to ask how the company is?"

"Uh, you think I would have." His brother's laughter sounded a little unhinged. "I'm sure Lacey has it all under control."

Dawson winced. Aaron had said he wasn't in love with his executive assistant, but stealing his number one employee would be just as bad, probably more so for someone like his money-grabbing, high-powered brother.

*Too bad, Lacey belongs to me.*

Aaron could keep the family name, his fancy cars, his mansion, over-priced clothes, and especially King Enterprises. Dawson found the real treasure. Lacey's love.

DEAR READER:

Thank you for taking the time to read Like a Boss. If you enjoyed it, please consider telling your friends or posting a short review. Word of mouth is an author's best friend and much appreciated.

Please signup for my newsletter at http://www.lizmatis.com

Coming Soon:

Aaron's story in Like a Drug - Double Trouble Duet - Book 2

Billionaire Aaron King could lose his company if stockholders discover his addiction. Forced into rehab he must rely on his estranged identical twin brother to pose as the CEO. Aaron is dedicated to regaining control of his life, but then he meets a woman he'll risk everything to possess.

County Music star Poppy Parker needs to be clean and sober before her world tour. Instead she gets dirty and drunk on a fellow rehab resident's body, which leads to an obsession that could risk her last chance at a comeback.

Are they trading one addiction for another? Or is it a love that can save them both?

# ABOUT THE AUTHOR

Liz Matis is a mild-mannered accountant by day and romance author by night. Married 30 years she believes in happily-ever-after!

Fun Fact: Liz read her first romance at the age of fifteen and soon after wrote her first romances starring her friends and their latest crushes!

Fun Fact 2: Liz keeps an inspiration board for all her books on Pinterest. Check it out here: http://www.pinterest.com/lizmatis/

**Keep in touch with Liz at:**

**Website:** http://www.lizmatis.com

**Blog:** http://www.taoofliz.blogspot.com

**Email:** elizabethmatis@gmail.com

**Twitter:** @LizMatis

**Facebook:**
https://www.facebook.com/LizMatisFanPage/

**Goodreads:**
http://www.goodreads.com/author/show/5289185.Liz_Matis

To sign up for my newsletter please see signup on via my website: http://www.lizmatis.com

**Liz Matis Reading List**

**The Complete Fantasy Football Romance Series Box Set**

From bestselling author, Liz Matis, comes the box set of the popular Fantasy Football Romance series! Includes the award-winning and #1 bestseller in Sports Fiction, **Playing For Keeps**, along with **Going For It** - also a #1 bestseller in Sports Fiction, **Huddle Up**, and **The Quarterback Sneak**, which also reached #1. The series has over 600 four and five stars reviews on Goodreads!

**Or start the series with Playing For Keeps**

Journalist Samantha Jameson always wanted to be one of the boys, but Ryan Terell won't let her join the club. Fresh from the battlegrounds of Iraq, reporting on a bunch of overgrown boys playing pro football is just the change of scenery she needs. If trying to be taken seriously in the world of sports writing wasn't hard enough, Ryan, her college crush, is only making it harder. As a tight-end for the team she's covering, he is strictly off limits.

Ryan Terell is a playmaker on and off the field, but when Samantha uncovers his moves, he throws out the playbook. Just as he claims his sweetest victory, Samantha's investigation into a steroid scandal involving his team forces him to call a time-out to their off the record trysts. But then a life threatening injury on the field will force them both to decide just how far they'll go to win the game.

Winner of the NECRWA First Kiss Contest.


## Summer Dreaming - Hot in the Hamptons
*I'm looking for a hero. Not.*

You'd think as a new college grad I'd be looking for the perfect job and the perfect man. Well, I'm not. Summer is here and instead of plotting my future, I'm playing in the Hamptons with my two best friends. Sun and sex is all I'm looking for. Then I meet Sean Dempsey, my fantasy lifeguard in the flesh. But he is more than just a hot bod with a whistle. And after he makes a daring save, I'm thinking a hero is exactly what I've been looking for all along.

*To the rescue...*

By day I guard the beaches in the Hamptons, by night I've had my fair share of summer flings. Then I meet Kelsey Mitchell, a girl with eyes like the setting sun and I burn for more. Something I have no right to ask of her...forever.


## Love By Design
Design Intervention starts the second season with its own surprise makeover. Interior designer Victoria

Bryce must break in her temporary co-host, Aussie Russ Rowland.

Sparks fly on camera as they argue over paint colors and measurement mishaps leading to passions igniting behind the scenes. But when their pasts collide with the present will the foundation they built withstand the final reveal? An HGTV meets Sex and the City romp!

**Real Men Don't Drink Appletinis**

Hollywood's handsomest men surround celebrity agent Ava Gardner but none are as intriguing as larger-than-life Grady O'Flynn. The Navy SEAL is on an unsanctioned mission when they end up starring in their own romantic comedy.

Will they continue to sizzle when Grady has to report back to duty? In this sexy novelette by Liz Matis, two lovers have two weeks to find out.

Made in the USA
Columbia, SC
16 October 2017